Shadow Hunters

Shadow Hunters Book One

E.J. King

PROLOGUE

They came at night. I had just crawled into bed and switched off the light. My sister was snoring softly in her bed across the room. It was the night before my first day of junior year and smiled at the thought of seeing my friends at school.

A loud pounding on the door of our apartment made my smile vanish. Nothing good ever accompanied a sound like that so late at night. I could hear my dad's heavy footsteps as he hurried to answer the door. Quietly, I tossed back my covers and crept across the room. I slid the door open, just a crack, so I could hear.

The voices were loud and urgent. My dad was being ordered to leave with the late-night visitors and he wasn't putting up much of a fight. A few seconds later, he came down the hall to wake us. I jumped back from the bedroom door just as it swung open.

"It's time to go," he said with a look in his eye that I had never seen.

We were allowed to pack a bag of basic necessities while we asked questions that he refused to answer. Less than ten minutes later, we were loaded into a car with dark windows and taken away from our home forever.

CHAPTER ONE

I watched the yellow dashes on the road as they sped past the car window. The sun had just appeared over the horizon and the sky was streaked with varying shades of pink and orange. Freshly harvested corn fields stretched endlessly and the only sound that could be heard was the gentle hum of the car's air conditioner.

As I shifted in my seat, I tugged at the seatbelt that was digging into my skin. We had been spending a lot of time in the car lately. A soft snore from the backseat signaled that my little brother, Tommy, had fallen asleep. I glanced over my shoulder and found him with his head tilted back and his mouth hanging open. His blond curls seemed to almost glow in the dark car interior. My sister, Madelyn, was pouting in the seat next to him. She was glaring out the window with headphones covering her ears to discourage any sort of conversation.

I sighed and turned back to the front. My dad was staring determinedly straight ahead as he clutched the steering wheel. "Almost there, kids," he announced without taking his eyes off the road.

A grimy road sign announced that we were entering Provenance, Iowa – population 42,543. The farmland had given way to sparsely populated city blocks. Dad continued to follow the black SUV leading us through town. We passed the local shopping mall, a handful of fast food restaurants, and a couple of parks. Not a single building stood over three stories tall. Eventually, we turned into a residential neighborhood and rolled to a stop in front of a two-story home. I unbuckled my seatbelt and climbed unsteadily from the car, my muscles tight from being in the car for five hours.

"Home sweet home," I muttered under my breath as I stretched my legs and took a closer look at the house. It had crisp white siding and a bright red door. The front porch held a rickety-looking swing and a new welcome mat. The grass had been freshly mowed and the shrubbery was neatly trimmed. To me, it looked like a house from a movie and not some place where anyone would actually live. Walking through the door felt like walking into my worst nightmare and it was about to get even worse – I still had to unpack.

"Hey, do you know where the towels are?" Madelyn asked a few hours later as she stood in the doorway to my new bedroom. Without looking up from the box I was unpacking, I shook my head and Madelyn turned sharply on her heels and stomped away. One the box was empty, I sat on the edge of my new bed and looked around the room.

The mahogany dresser was position to the left of the door with two of its drawers still open, revealing the meager contents inside. An old, scuffed and dented desk stood opposite the dresser, just underneath the window which looked over the front of the house. The bed was covered in a bright, floral bedspread that hurt your eyes if you looked at it very long. A small table next to the bed held just three items: a small lamp, an alarm clock, and a silver framed photograph. It was the only personal touch in the room.

The photograph had been taken was I was just eight-years-old and I was smiling up at a beautiful woman with flowing blond hair and sparkling green eyes. At a distance, that flawless woman looked utterly angelic. Unfortunately, my mother had been undeniably mortal and anything but flawless.

I rose from the bed and wandered over to the window. It had an unobstructed view of the idyllic-looking neighborhood. A couple small children were riding their bikes up and down the sidewalk. Next door, a neighbor was watering his lawn and further down the street, a lawnmower was humming. It was a drastically different environment than the congestion and skyscrapers I was used to seeing outside my window.

One last box sat on the edge of my bed waiting to be unpacked. I flipped open the lid and was greeted by my own face staring back at me. It was a snapshot of me and my two best friends, Chloe and Annabeth, and had been taken in my bedroom back in New York. We were mugging at the camera with huge grins, dressed in our navy-blue school uniforms. My blond hair was down and it flowed well past my shoulders.

With a bit of hesitation, I allowed my eyes to find the mirror above the dresser. The reflection that stared back at me looked nothing like the happy teenager in the photo. The bond hair had been replaced with a shorter style and had been dyed red. The smile from the photo had been transformed into a grimace and the green eyes no longer shined. I regretted looking in the mirror and contemplated getting rid of it completely.

Instead, I focused on the second picture in the box. In that photo, I was still smiling but this time the smile was directed at a handsome boy wearing a suit. It had been taken at last year's prom. Josh, the boy in the suit, had been my first serious boyfriend. The relationship had ended abruptly when I was forced to leave, not even given the chance to say goodbye to him.

More memories of my old life were buried deeper in the box: varsity letters for tennis and basketball, more photos, concert tickets, museum brochures, and a Kent Academy student ID. My whole life was neatly tucked away in a small cardboard box.

Feeling a wave of depression coming, I tossed everything back into the box and shoved it as far back in the closet as it would go. After shutting the door, I glanced at the stack of school books perched precariously on the edge of the desk. English, Spanish, history, chemistry, and trigonometry. A couple of those classes would be repeats for me since I had taken advanced classes at my old school. I wouldn't even be able to distract myself from my misery by throwing myself into my school work.

I took one last look around to make sure everything was put away and then headed downstairs to help unpack the rest of the house. It took almost six hours to get everything put away. Tommy was only eight years old, so he needed a lot of help unpacking. We had brought very few of our own possessions, but a lot of other things had been supplied for us and still needed to be put away. By the time the last box had been emptied, I was exhausted.

Back in my room, I turned on a television that as at least ten years old. I flipped through the channels until I found a mindless sitcom and tried to think of anything other than my present situation. The doorbell rang and I heard Dad's footsteps on the stairs. Considering that we didn't know anyone in town, I had a pretty good hunch who was at the door. That hunch was confirmed a minute later when I was called downstairs.

I was the last one to enter the living room. Tommy was playing a video game and Madelyn was messing around with her new cell phone. Dad was pacing nervously around the room and another man stood rigidly in the corner, watching us all. I wasn't the least bit surprised to find him lurking in the shadows of our new house.

I took a seat on the couch and tucked my legs beneath me. Dad nodded his head at the other man. "Kids, you remember Deputy Marshal Taylor?"

Madelyn and I nodded mutely and Tommy offered a timid, "Yes."

"Call me Jim, please," he said, stepping into the center of the room. Tommy put down his game and Madelyn looked up from her phone.

"Jim is here to go over some important stuff for tomorrow, so pay attention." Dad took a seat on the other end of the couch. His face looked even more tense than usual and his eyes were bloodshot from lack of sleep.

"Tomorrow is a very important day for all of you," Jim said. "It is absolutely vital that you not make any mistakes. Try not to share too many details about your former lives. The less you say, the less likely you will be to slip up and say the wrong thing.

"Of course, you know that you must only use your new names. Never, ever use your old names. It's a risk that you cannot afford to take."

Jim looked each of us in the eye to make sure we understood the important of his words. I saw Tommy's lower lip begin to tremble and I could tell that he was frightened. "The federal witness protection program only works if you respect the rules We have never lost a protectee who follows the rules."

I didn't need to ask for an explanation of what he meant by "lost."

"Your old names – Paul, Alex, Madelyn, and Tommy Garretty – are gone for good. From now on, you will only use the names Clark, Allyson, Madison, and Peter Wilson. If anyone asks, you are from St. Louis and your mother, Mary, died in a car accident eight years ago."

It was hard to hear Jim make up lies about my mother.

"Allyson and Madison will be attending Provenance High School as a junior and freshman respectively. Peter will be in third grade at Provenance Elementary. Clark, as you know, we've set you up with a job at a local insurance company. As far as anyone knows, you've only ever worked in insurance. No one will ever know that you were once a federal agent. Also, you should not access your old email accounts or social media sights. Don't email, call, or write letters to former friends. That would be a serious breach of security."

"This sucks," Madelyn muttered as she slumped in her seat.

"Madelyn–" Dad started to scold her, but Jim held up a hand.

"Yes, it does suck," Jim agreed as he turned to Madelyn. "But it's better than ending up dead."

Jim took a deep breath. "I know this is a very difficult situation for all of you, but the witness protection rules exist to keep you safe."

I was still having a hard time accepting the phrase "witness protection" as part of my everyday vocabulary. During the big move, we had each been given a handbook of rules along with a detailed accounting of our new identities, all of which we had to memorize. The last few weeks had been a blur of disbelief.

Jim continued to tell us to forget everything we had ever known, including things I had no intention of ever forgetting. But I also knew that we were being hunted by violent, evil people and those people would kill me or any member of my family without giving it a second thought. Even if I hated this new life with every fiber of my being, I would suck it up and become Ally Wilson.

I woke early the next morning, hours before my alarm clock rang out and pierced the early-morning quiet Normally, the first day of school excited me. But nothing about this new life was normal. In the shower, I practiced saying my new name out loud, hoping it would become more natural. "Allyson. Ally. Ally Wilson."

Because Dad had been a federal agent with valuable information about an incredibly powerful and dangerous man, the U.S. Marshals had decided not to take any chances. We had been buried deep in the program and everything about us had been changed, including our names and physical appearances.

After my shower, I picked out a pair of designer jeans and a plain black t-shirt. I had no idea how teenagers in Iowa dressed for school, but jeans and a t-shirt seemed safe enough. I slide on a pair of silver flip flops and ran a brush through my hair before heading downstairs for breakfast.

A note on the table said that Dad had already left for work and was dropping Tommy at his school on the way. Next to the note was a sheet of paper with detailed instructions on how to get to the high school with a set of keys on top of it, presumably for the car I would be driving to school. I was feeling too anxious to eat, so I nibbled on a banana while I waited for Madelyn to come downstairs.

When Madelyn finally made an appearance, she was wearing a short summer dress and gold sandals. Her long, dark hair was arranged in elaborate curls and she had applied heavy eyeliner to accent the green in her eyes. She barely resembled the sister that I had shared a room with for fourteen years.

The sun was shining brightly when we stepped outside and I slipped a pair of sunglasses from my backpack. We would be arriving at school in style in a Toyota from the late nineties. I had only recently obtained a driver's license and rarely had a reason to drive in the city, so I was nervous as I started the car.

Most of Provenance could be accessed by driving a few miles in either direction down the main road, conveniently called Main Street. We took the road for about a mile before taking a right onto York Street. The high school was just two blocks from Main Street and the entire drive took less than five minutes.

The school was quite unremarkable. The two-story structure had clearly been built sometime in the 1970s and along with the football field, baseball diamond, and tennis courts, it encompassed just one square block. Students wearing matching athletic attire were running on the track around the football field. Other students were spread out on picnic tables near the front entrance.

I could feel the students watching us as we walked toward the front door. It felt a lot like walking a plank. Most of the eyes passed right over me and landed on Madelyn who was marking with her shoulders back and her head held high.

We headed to the administrative office where a woman greeted us with a smile and a snap of pink bubblegum. The nameplate on the desk said she was Miss Copland. Madelyn approached her with a sweet smile and a toss of her hair.

"We're the Wilson sisters. Today is our first day." Madelyn said the name Wilson perfectly.

"Oh, of course!" Miss Copland smiled widely and pulled a stack of manila folders from her desk. She thumbed through them quickly and retrieved two from the middle. "Okay, which of you is Allyson?"

There was an uncomfortable silence as I failed to recognize my new name. Madelyn jumped in. "I'm Maddy. That's Ally."

"Great." She handed us each a folder with our names neatly printed on them. "Inside those folders you will find a map of the school, your schedules, locker information, school rules and regulations, the school fight song, and other important information. Take some time to look it all over and come find me if you have any questions."

"She seems sweet," Madelyn said when we were out of earshot. I rolled my eyes, not at all surprised that my cheerleader sister was charmed by Miss Peppy.

"Our lockers are that way," I said, heading down the hallway. We passed a few students in the hall and they were all staring with open curiosity. It was clear that Provenance High didn't get a lot of new students. At the end of the hallway, we entered a large square lobby surrounded by lockers. The room was packed with teenagers scrambling to gather their books, finish their homework, and catch up with friends. I turned to say something to Madelyn and found that I was alone. She had already disappeared into the crowd.

My locker, number 336, was hidden in a corner right next to the door for classroom 11. I shoved my books inside and retrieved my class schedule and the school map. Coincidentally, my homeroom was in room 11. Just as I was about to enter the room, a flurry of activity caught my eye. When I turned around, I found Madelyn surrounded by a gaggle of young girls. They were all talking and laughing like they had been best friends for years. I wasn't surprised. It was no secret that she had always been the more outgoing Garretty sister. Madelyn was friendlier, more charming, more flirtatious, and more beautiful.

I had always struggled more to fit in. At Kent Academy, it had been easier. I had known most of my classmates there since we were young kids and I'd established a core group of close friends. I had been popular because I got good grades, was a decent athlete, and had a strong sense of humor. I had been part of the yearbook staff and on the student council. My popularity had been earned by a lot of hard work and it was going to take a long time for me to find my place in this new school.

Most of the seats in the classroom were already taken and the students stared at me as I entered the room. I offered a shy smile before approaching an older gentleman at the teacher's desk. He was leaning back in his chair with his feet propped on the desk while reading a newspaper. When I approached, he peered over the top of the paper at me.

"Allyson Wilson, I presume?" His tone had just a hint of annoyance.

"Yes, sir."

"I'm Mr. Craig. You can have a seat in the middle row, second seat from the back."

I headed straight to my seat and avoided making eye contact with anyone. I could hear whispers as I passed. Two empty seats remained when the bell rang, one directly behind me and on immediately to my left. Mr. Craig put his newspaper down and picked up the attendance seat just as the two missing students arrived.

The first tardy student was a petite girl with short, spiky pink hair who wore heavy eyeliner and a nose-ring. The second student was the exact opposite of her. He was tall, several inches over six foot, with a strong jaw and chiseled cheekbones. His eyes were darker than any I had ever seen and he carried himself with a confidence that was virtually inexistent in teenagers. None of these things on their own was remarkable, but the combination of all of them was mesmerizing.

He moved gracefully across the room with his broad shoulders pushed back. I found myself staring at him, just like all the other females in the room. His eyes caught mine and he smiled, a crooked and unconvincing smile that would have seemed disingenuous on anyone else. On him, it was charming.

Annoyed that I could feel myself blushing, I turned away quickly and directed my eyes to my desk where I began doodling intensely on my notebook cover. Mr. Craig continued his roll call, moving down the roster without looking up.

"Betsy Schoel?"

"Here."

"Pam Seal?"

"Yeah."

"Daniel Stevens?

"Present," said my new neighbor in a low voice.

Mr. Craig finished his list and then added a name, "Allyson Wilson?"

"Here?" It came out more as a question than a statement of fact. Heads swiveled as late arrivers got their first looks at the new girl. I ducked my head and hoped that everyone would grow bored quickly. Mr. Craig turned back to his paper and the students eventually began chatting with one another about their weekends. I could feel Daniel's eyes still on me, waiting for an opening to strike up a conversation, or perhaps, an inquisition. He finally gave up and turned his attention to the blond boy in front of him, asking about an English paper that was due.

Another bell rang signaling the end of homeroom and I stayed in my seat while the other students hurried off to first period. My history class was in the same room and I wasn't sure if I should stay in the same seat or not. I fidgeted uncomfortably as I tried to decide if I should move.

"You can stay there. No one sits in that seat," Daniel said, as if reading my mind. His voice sent a chill down my spine.

"Thanks," I muttered.

"You're welcome." He paused for a beat. "Nice drawing. Are you an artist?"

"I… what?" I glanced over and noticed that his eyes were on my notebook. When I followed their trajectory, I was surprised by what I saw. In the ten minutes of my mindless doodling, I had drawn a surprisingly good likeness of a demon. I had included horns, fangs, and fiery eyes. I didn't even remember drawing it, but there it was looking up at me.

"It's just a doodle," I said unconvincingly.

"So, Allyson Wilson, where are you from?" Daniel wasn't going to let me off the hook yet, apparently.

"St. Louis," I lied awkwardly. "We just moved to town this weekend for my dad's job. You can call me Ally."

When I looked at Daniel, I wasn't sure my lies had been convincing. His eyes were narrowed slightly as they peered intently into my own. I told myself that he couldn't possibly know I was lying, but I felt another chill shoot through my body. I was just feeling paranoid. Then the moment was over and Daniel gave me another of his crooked smiles.

"St. Louis, huh? The city with the arch?" he said. I noticed that his eyes weren't actually black, but a very dark blue. "Did you like it there?"

I kept my answer as vague as possible. "Yeah, it was fine. I miss my friends."

"Understandable. My family just moved to town, too, about a month ago. I'm from Idaho." His smile turned sympathetic.

"Idaho? The state with the potatoes?" I asked dryly and Daniel laughed.

We chatted until the bell rang and first period began. It was nice to know that someone understood how I felt being the new kid. I was able to relax with Daniel, almost like he was an old friend. For a second, I almost forgot that I wasn't Alex Garretty anymore. I just felt like me again.

CHAPTER TWO

After history, I had Spanish class with Senorita Diaz. She was a young woman and very engaging but best of all, she briefly introduced me to the class in Spanish and then let me take a seat in the back. When class was over, I ducked into the bathroom to pass the five minutes before my next class, English.

Three girls had commandeered the sinks and mirrors. Two of the girls stood quietly, checking their makeup and fixing their hair. The third girl was telling them about her latest shopping spree with her father's credit card.

"I mean, they were only $200 and I totally needed new sunglasses. So whatever, I bought them and-" She stopped and her reflection in the mirror cocked an eyebrow at me. "You're the new girl, right?"

"Ally," I said, offering my most sociable smile. The girl turned on her heel, sending her blond mane of hair flying, and she offered me a smile of her own that revealed perfect, sparkling teeth.

"I love your jeans. So chic. Where did you get them?"

"This little boutique in Soho," I replied without thinking. I nearly slapped a hand over my mouth when I realized my mistake. "My family vacationed in New York over the summer."

"That's cool. I'm Talya and this is Kami and Lexi."
She pointed to each girl. Kami, the girl with the over-
highlighted hair smiled tightly and Lexi waved a perfectly
manicured hand in my general vicinity. "What class do you
have next?"

"Um… English. With Mrs. Parker," I said after
glancing at the schedule clutched in my hand.

"Awesome. We have the same class. Let's walk."
Talya led the way out of the bathroom with Kami and Lexi
close at her heels. She talked the entire way to class and
didn't stop until the bell rang, pausing only long enough to
introduce me to Mrs. Parker. After showing me to an
empty desk next to hers, Talya jumped right back into her
story about her favorite shade of nail polish. I was amazed
at her ability to talk so incessantly without saying anything.

When class started, I leaned back and let out a sigh of
relief. The sound of soft chuckling made me glance over
my shoulder. Daniel was there, slouched in his seat and
smiling knowingly. I returned his smile as Mrs. Parker
began her lecture.

English class quickly became my favorite class of the
day. I sat quietly as everyone around me offered their
opinions freely on the symbolism in *Catcher in the Rye*. Even
Talya participated, explaining the reasons why Holden was

nothing more than an antisocial freak.

"Please, he was so emo," she said as she filed down her nails.

Before I knew it, class was over and it was time for lunch. I dreaded walking into the cafeteria alone, but that was my only option other than not eating at all. I found the cafeteria after making just two wrong turns and grabbed a salad and a bottle of water from the lunch line. Looking around the room, I tried to find an acceptable place to sit.

Talya and her cult of wannabes were seated at a large table in the middle of the room. I saw Daniel seated a smaller table in the corner with a group of athletic looking boys. Madelyn was at the center of a large crowd of younger teens near the windows. Nobody seemed to notice me as I circled around uncertainly.

Just as I was about to give up hope of ever finding a seat, I noticed a set of open glass doors leading to an outdoor patio area. I was about to pass through the doorway when another person stepped directly in front of me. I put one hand out to stop my momentum and somehow managed to push the guy to the ground.

"Ahhh!" My victim cried out as he tumbled backward out the doors and landed on the concrete. His tray of food flew into the air and landed directly on his head. The cafeteria erupted with mocking applause and my face flushed with warmth.

"Holy crap. I'm so so so so sorry," I said as I reached down to help him up.

He looked up at me with a sheepish smile. "My bad," he said as he pulled a French fry from his hair and tossed it onto his tray. He grabbed my hand and I pulled him to his feet. Despite how easily I had knocked him over, he was surprisingly solid in build and slightly taller than my 5'9" height.

"Are you sure you're okay? I feel terrible about this. I really should have been watching were I was going." I dusted some crumbs off his shirt.

"It was totally worth it to get a pretty girl to touch me," he joked as he wiped his face off with a napkin. He tossed his now empty tray on top of a nearby trashcan. "Were you looking for a place to sit?"

"Yeah."

"Well, I can say quite confidently that the ground out here is more comfortable that you might expect," he said with a laugh.

"Good to know." I noticed that when he laughed, even his eyes seemed to be laughing.

Follow me, my lady," he said making a grand gesture with his arm. I followed him through the crowd to a table that was occupied by a lone girl who was laughing openly as we approached.

"Smooth, Bax," she said as he slid into an empty seat. "The fries are a good look for you."

"I can make anything look good." He helped himself to a bite of the girl's sandwich. "Cadence, this is New Girl. New Girl, this is Cadence."

"It's Ally, actually." I set my salad on the table and took a seat across from Cadence.

"Hi, Ally," she said with a warm smile. "Don't mind Baxter. Not everyone in this school is as clumsy as him."

"Ha. Ha," Baxter said slowly through a mouthful of Cadence's lunch.

"Thanks for letting me sit with you. I was beginning to think I might have to eat by myself and be established as a weird loner on my very first day." I made a half-hearted attempt to enjoy my salad, but my stomach was still in knots.

"Well, you picked the right loser to knock down," Cadence said, swatting away Baxter's hand just as he was about to swipe the last of her fries. "This is pretty much the best table."

"This is true. If you were hoping to become immediate best friends with the two most unremarkable and easily forgettable people in the school, you have succeeded," Baxter said.

"Perfect. Mission accomplished," I said with a relieved smile. Baxter and Cadence were nothing like my old friends, but I was beginning to realize that wasn't necessarily a bad thing.

"I promise, we aren't completely pathetic." Cadence smiled sheepishly.

"That's right. Cade is the top swimmer in school, which would be some serious clout if anyone at this school actually knew that we have a swim team."

"And Baxter is amazing at crashing into people and falling down, which works out pretty well for him when he's man-handling opponents on the wrestling mats." Cadence and Baxter seemed to have a knack for teasing one another and I got the feeling they had been friends for quite some time.

"Well it sounds like I'm in good company," I said as I took a long swig of water.

"You could do much worse," Baxter agreed. "For instance, you could have sat at that table there with the incredibly beautiful and popular people. Or you could have sat over there with the future doctors and rocket scientists. Just imagine how miserable you would be."

They spent the entire lunch hour joking like that, making fun of one another and occasionally revealing pertinent personal information. Cadence and Baxter learned the basics about me– name, age, hometown, siblings. All the information was tailored to my new identity, of course, and I learned the same about both of them.

I wasn't even aware it was happening, but suddenly I had friends again. Maybe they were quirky and sat far away from the popular crowd, but I was okay with that because they didn't seem to mind at all that I was being quiet and reserved. I was still learning how to be around people again, but it was turning out to be just like riding a bike, or getting back on the horse. Insert the appropriate cliché here.

It turned out that Cadence and I had almost all the same afternoon classes, so we walked to trigonometry together. She led us up to the second floor and down a dark hallway. The room was full by the time we arrived and there were only two empty seats left in the front row. Cadence introduced me to Mr. Smythe and as I was taking my seat, I noticed Daniel in the back row. I returned his wave with a small one of my own.

"You know Daniel?" Cadence asked once we were seated.

"Not really. We had some classes together this morning." I opened my notebook and scribbled down the date. "We sort of bonded over being new here."

"He was new like a month ago," Cadence whispered. "Now it's almost like he's always been here."

"How do you mean?" I risked a glance over my shoulder. Daniel was laughing at something the girl in front of him had said. That girl happened to be Talya.

"It's kind of typical really. He moves here with his family at the beginning of the school year. Within a couple of weeks, he and his sister are the most well-known people in school." Cadence dug in her book bag for a pencil. "People even know all about their older brother and he's not even in high school anymore."

"All three of them? That's kind of odd." I thought about how my own sister had become part of the popular crowd in half a day and knew I wouldn't be joining Madelyn in the inner circle anytime soon.

"It might have something to do with the fact that they are all attractive, smart, friendly, and worst of all," Cadence looked at Daniel briefly and then turned back to me, "they are genuinely nice. That's pretty much unheard of in this school."

"The nerve of some people…" I whispered and shook my head, feigning annoyance.

"Class, open your books to page 30 and begin working on problems one through four." Mr. Smythe interrupted our gossiping and we both concentrated on solving trigonometry problems for the rest of class. When class was over, we resumed chatting as we gathered our books.

"Hi, Ally," Talya said as she walked past. She gave me a big smile and glanced at Cadence. Her face twitched just a little and her smile faded. "How's your first day going?"

"Well I'm still alive so I'd say so far so good." It was supposed to be a joke, but it was also a little true. Talya's smile faltered again and she hesitated before responding.

"Great. Well, I'll see you around." She scampered off and Cadence laughed.

"Guess I won't be invited to her next slumber party," I said as I stood and tossed my bag over my shoulder.

"You might want to consider taking Pep 101. That's where they teach them to plaster those fake smiles on their faces and say peppy things all day." Cadence followed me out of the room.

"And here all this time I thought that's why they created cheerleading squads," I said. Cadence led me down the hall to our next class, chemistry. The science labs were at the other end of the building and we had to weave our way through a maze of students.

The chemistry room was made up of ten different lab stations with two or three students assigned to each station. Cadence took her seat next to her lab partners and Mr. Fuller pointed me to another station with an empty seat. I introduced myself to my new lab partners. The quiet girl with glasses was named Maya and the guy seated next to her was the exact opposite. His name was Billy Jenkins and he spent the entire glass goofing around and telling jokes.

There was one scary moment where Billy mixed the wrong chemicals and caused the beaker to overflow but other than that, I considered chemistry class to be a success. After class, Cadence walked me to the gym even though her last class of the day was in the art room. She seemed to have taken over the responsibility of showing me the ropes. She even went so far as to introduce me to the gym instructor, Mr. Thompson, who preferred for his students to call him Mr. T.

I bit my lip against all "pity the fool" jokes and accepted the gym clothes he offered me. Most of the girls in the locker room had already changed into their navy shorts and gray Provenance Panthers t-shirts. I changed quickly and hurried to catch up with them and found Baxter out on the gym floor, attempting unsuccessfully to spin a basketball on his finger.

"Mr. T isn't a big fan of organized athletic training, which makes this job just perfect for him. Right now, we are all playing Pig." Baxter shot his ball at the nearest rim where it clanked loudly before bouncing off and hitting Mr. T in the back of the head.

The class was divided into six teams of four and we were each assigned to a basketball hoop. My group was made up of one girl who refrained from playing by volunteering to chase down all the misses, a tall boy who couldn't hit a shot five feet away from the basket, and a tough looking girl who took the game way too seriously. I heard Mr. T call her Leah and I was a little frightened when the girl marched toward me after our game.

"You're good." She said the words with hostility and eyed me with contempt. "How tall are you?"

"5'9"," I replied, trying not to sound worried. I had a hunch why Leah wanted to know that information.

"You didn't miss a single shot today. Did you play basketball at your old school?"

"Sort of," I said, unsure if this was a time to tell the truth or if a lie would get me better results.

"You should try out for the team. We need another tall girl that can shoot," said Leah.

"That?" I said, referencing my flawless performance. "That was just luck. I never make shots like that normally."

Mr. T saved me from further interrogation when he

came over to record our results. Leah stared me down one last time as she walked away. A couple of other teams were still finishing up, so I headed over to the bleachers to watch.

"Ally, heads up!"

I turned my head and threw up my hands just in time to catch the basketball that was headed toward my nose. The ball made a satisfying smack as it collided with my palms.

"You've got quick reflexes," Billy said as he jogged over to retrieve his ball.

"Nice shot, Ace," I replied, lobbying the ball at him. He caught it with a grin and headed back to his game. I checked my hands and found that the index finger on my right hand was slightly swollen and bruised. I could move it, though somewhat painfully, but at least it wasn't broken. I must have jammed it when I caught the ball.

"You alright?" Daniel said, appearing from nowhere.

"Yeah. I just jammed my finger. No biggie," I said, flexing my finger slowly. Daniel stood in front of me with his hand outstretched.

"May I?" he asked, reaching for my hand. I nodded and he pinched my finger between his index finger and thumb, applying slight pressure to the knuckle. I expected to feel pain, but instead there was just a rush of warmth at the sight of the injury. Daniel kept his grip for a few more seconds and then let go.

"Better?"

I tried moving my finger and found that it bent easily with no pain. The swelling seemed to be receding as well.

"Actually, yes. How did you do that?"

"One thing you should know about me," Daniel said with a smile, "I have a lot of useful skills."

Mr. T conveniently blew his whistle just then and everyone headed off to the locker rooms. After I changed, I still had to run back to my locker to grab my books and car keys. I was surprised to find Madelyn standing by my locker, arms crossed and foot tapping the floor impatiently.

"Finally. Geez." She flicked her hair over her shoulder and gave me one of her famous Madelyn-looks.

"What's up, sis?" I asked in a sugary voice. Killing Madelyn with kindness was one of my favorite pastimes.

"I just wanted to tell you that I don't need a ride home. I have cheer practice and Lily is giving me a ride home afterwards." She adjusted the strap of her book bag and waved to where some of her new friends were gathered.

"Cheer practice? Already?" I shook my head in disbelief as I twirled the combination on my locker.

"Whatever. Fine. See you at home later."

Madelyn skipped off to join her friends and they all squealed and giggled as they walked away. I tried not to be annoyed at how easily she had managed to fit in. I really did want my sister to be happy.

The parking lot was almost half-empty when I walked outside. Most of the cars that were still there belonged to students who participated in after school activities and I wondered if I should join a club or something just to have somewhere to belong on a regular basis. Or maybe I should take Leah up on her offer and join the basketball team.

"New girl, wait up!"

I spun around and found Baxter jogging in my direction. He was wearing his goofy grin and a Kansas City Royals baseball hat. "What's up, Bax?" I was surprised at how easily his nickname rolled off my tongue.

"I'm supposed to meet Cadence at Java Café for some study action. You should join us. I hear you're a trig guru," he said as we headed across the parking lot.

"I don't know about that. But I could go for a mocha," I said.

"Excellent. This is my car here. Want to just follow me?" Baxter tossed his bag into the backseat.

I agreed to follow him and walked toward my car,

stopping for a second to look around. I could have sworn that someone was watching me, but when I spun in a circle there was no one around. I shook away the feeling and climbed into my car, but not before checking to make sure no one was lurking in the backseat.

CHAPTER THREE

The combination of three teenagers and a bunch of caffeine wasn't exactly conducive to getting much studying done. On the plus side, by the time I left to go home for dinner, I felt comfortable referring to Cadence and Baxter as my friends.

That night, my family gathered around the dinner table and pretended we were just a normal family decompressing after the first day at school. Tommy couldn't stop talking about his new school and friends. One of the boys in his class had snakes for pets and Tommy couldn't wait to go over to his house and play with them. Madelyn chatted happily about her new cheerleader friends and I even mentioned my afternoon with Cadence and Baxter.

Dad seemed relieved that we were all adjusting so well, or at least that we were all really good at pretending. He was also glad that none of us had any slipups to report. He didn't talk much about his new job, preferring to let the kids do the talking. I knew it had to be hard to go from being an FBI agent to selling insurance, but I also knew that Dad would do anything to keep his children safe.

I slept soundly that night for the first time in weeks.

Ever since our lives had been uprooted, my sleep had been getting interrupted by nightmares of being hunted and killed by evil men lurking in dark alleyways. The solid eight hours of sleep was utterly refreshing.

In homeroom, Daniel was even more talkative than the day before. This time, his topic of discussion was weekend plans. He was trying to convince me to attend a party at my lab partner's house.

"There is absolutely no better way to get to know your classmates than to watch them hooking up with random people and throwing up in bushes," Daniel said. I was trying to read about the Boston Tea Party in preparation for our next class, but Daniel wouldn't let me focus.

"Gee, that does sound like a hoot. I can't imagine why someone would be reluctant to witness that." I reread the same sentence for the fourth time and tried not to let Daniel see that my resolve was wearing down.

"Well, not to mention the fact that I'll be there. That right there should seal the deal." Daniel reached over and shut my book, forcing me to look at him. I tried to give him my fiercest stare, but I ended up smiling instead.

"I'll think about it," I conceded.

"Excellent. The party is starting at seven, but I really think it won't get interesting until at least nine."

"I didn't say yes. I said I would think about it," I said, but I knew that Daniel would only hear what he wanted to hear. "I need to check with Cadence and Baxter. We're supposed to hang out this weekend."

"No worries. They're going to the party, too. Everyone will be there." Daniel sat back with a satisfied smile on his face.

At lunch, Cadence and Baxter confirmed that we would be attending Billy's party. We planned to go together, partly because I had no idea where Billy lived and also because Baxter was an advocate of strength in numbers.

I was nervous as I got ready for the party Friday night. Tommy was hanging out on my bed, watching me bounce around the room. I was pulling clothes from my closet, trying to figure out what to wear.

"Where are you going?" Tommy asked as I tossed down another reject from the closet. The pile at my feet was growing at an alarming rate.

"To a party. At a friend's house." I knew Billy wasn't technically a friend, but no need splitting hairs.

"What will you do there? Play games? When I go to parties for my friends we play games and eat cake. Will there be cake?" Tommy was in a talkative mood and his questions were a perfect distraction.

"Probably not. I suppose there might be games." I frowned, thinking about the rumors I had heard about drinking games. "What are you going to do tonight?"

"I dunno. Can I go with you?" Tommy looked at me so hopefully that I almost agreed.

"Sorry, kiddo. You can't come tonight. But we can hang out tomorrow night."

"Promise?"

"Absolutely. We can do whatever you want." I ruffled his blond curls and thought about how sad I would be when he grew up and didn't want to hang out with his sister anymore.

Once Tommy had gone off to his room to play video games, I settled on an outfit– a short navy blue t-shirt dress and gold flip flops. I brushed my hair until it shone and was slicking on some lip gloss when I heard a car horn blast outside. Cadence had offered to pick me up for the party, so I grabbed my purse and skipped downstairs.

"You. Stop right there," Dad called out as my hand was about to turn the doorknob.

"Yes, Father?" I backpedaled to the living room where he was watching a baseball game on television.

"You will be home by midnight?" Dad said as he fixed me with a stern glare.

"Of course." I tried not to roll my eyes. Cadence

sounded her horn again. "Can I go now?"

"Just a second. I would like to remind you that you are not allowed to drink tonight. I know you are going to some party, but you need to be responsible."

"Dad, I know." This time I didn't fight the urge to let my eyes roll.

"I mean it. Stop with the snotty teenager eye rolling. You have to be extra careful about what you say and do tonight. You can't afford to make any mistakes." I had never heard Dad sound so serious.

"Okay. I promise to be extra careful, Pops." I gave him my most responsible-daughter look and he gave me a satisfied nod. I assumed that meant I was dismissed and left quickly before he could change his mind.

"You look great," Cadence said as I slid into the car.

I squirmed in my seat and tugged down the hem of my dress. I was still getting used to how people dressed in Provenance. It hadn't been uncommon for my old friends to get dressed up for parties, but I noticed that Cadence was wearing a simple pair of jeans and a Led Zeppelin t-shirt. Her shiny hair was slicked back in a high ponytail and her face was free of makeup. She looked natural and confident.

"Thanks. You look nice, too," I said. Baxter's house was just a few blocks from my new house, so it took no time at all to swing by and pick him up. He slid into the backseat, made some borderline comments about how "nice" the girls looked, and they were off to the party.

Aside from being a terrible lab partner in chemistry, Bill Jenkins was also the son of one of the richest men in town. He lived in a subdivision sparsely populated with lavish homes. Cadence parked in front of the biggest of those homes and already several teenagers could be seen hanging out on the front porch.

"Shall we ladies?" Baxter asked and we followed him from the car to the front door. A few people called a greeting in our direction, but I didn't recognize any of them. The door was wide open, so we walked into the foyer. More teenagers milled about, talking and drinking from red plastic cups. Somewhere in the house, the base of a stereo was thumping.

We worked our way further into the house. As I made a final push through the crowd and into the kitchen, I suddenly became aware that I had been separated from Cadence and Baxter. I looked around hopelessly, feeling exposed and alone in a room full of people.

"I knew you couldn't resist my charms," Daniel said as he sidled up next to me. "You here alone?"

"Hardly. I came with friends. I'm just… lost." I gave a helpless laugh.

"Well good thing I found you then." Daniel held out a hand. "Would you come with me, please? There are people I would like you to meet."

I hesitated for only a second before slipping my hand into his. He guided me through the crowd toward a set of sliding glass doors that took us outside. Daniel led the way across the deck to where a group of teens was lounging in the corner. They stopped talking and eyed me curiously.

Daniel nonchalantly dropped my hand and began a round of introductions. My eyes were immediately drawn to one of the guys in the center of the group. He was leaning comfortably against the questionable looking railing and he appraised me with narrowed eyes.

"This is my brother, Elliot," Daniel said.

"Please, call me Eli. Elliot sounds so pretentious, don't you think?" he said as he dragged himself from his relaxed pose. Once completely vertical, I saw that he was nearly as tall as his brother, but that was where the physical similarities ended. Where Daniel was lean and fit, Eli was broad and strong. His hair was a spectacular shade of golden blond and flopped carelessly over his eyes. Those eyes. They were a striking shade of icy blue.

A petite girl standing next to Eli smiled and offered me her hand. Her short hair was pitch black and stuck out in dangerous points. "Hey. I'm Lily. I'm Daniel and Eli's sister."

"Nice to meet you, Lily." I was surprised at the strength behind the tiny girl's handshake, but I managed to return her warm smile with a nervous one of my own.

Despite my initial impression of Eli as being cool and detached, it wasn't long before his self-deprecating humor won me over. Still, it felt like he occasionally looked at me too intensely and sometimes his gaze seemed to linger too long, but I was probably just being paranoid.

I was laughing at something Daniel had said when a movement from the door behind him caught my eye. There, with his face pressed against the glass in an unflattering manner, was my new friend, Baxter. Cadence was also there, shaking her head in disgust. She made eye contact with me and we both laughed, causing Daniel to give me a perplexed look.

"I'm sorry." I stifled my laughter, but not before Daniel figured out that something was happening behind him. He turned around just as Baxter pushed himself away from the window too quickly and crashed into Talya, who just happened to be walking behind him at that very moment. The collision knocked her into the wall and most of her drink flew straight up before cascading to the floor. Baxter was still trying to regain his balance and his foot slipped on the liquid, sending him to the floor. Talya responded by throwing her remaining drink in Baxter's face.

"I, um, I'll be back," I told Daniel as I hurried inside to protect Baxter from Talya's wrath.

"Need some help?" Daniel called after me, trying to hold back his laughter.

"Thanks, but I've got it," I said with a laugh of my own. "I'm sure her bark is worse than her bite."

"Do you have any idea how much this cardigan cost?" Talya was asking Baxter, who was still seated on the floor. "This is cashmere. And now you've ruined it!"

"I'm really, really sorry," Baxter apologized, but I could see the laughter dancing in his eyes.

"You'll pay for this!" Talya swore before she stomped away.

"Smooth, Bax. Real smooth." I offered him a hand.

He climbed to his feet. "I do what I can," he joked. "Think she'll ever forgive me?"

"I doubt she'll even remember it in the morning," I assured him. "But if she does, you're screwed."

"Great. Thanks. That's very reassuring." Baxter grabbed a kitchen towel that Cadence offered him and began mopping off his face and hair.

"Having fun?" I asked Cadence.

"Oh, is that what this is called?" she said. We stepped

away from the mess on the floor and found some space to stand in the living room.

I talked to Cadence and Baxter for almost half an hour before I remembered how hastily I had abandoned Daniel and the others outside. After making Baxter promise not to cause any more commotions, I headed back outside to find Daniel. I found him just where I had left him, out back talking with Eli. The others had disappeared now and it was just the two of them, engrossed in an intense conversation. I stopped just inside the doorway and listened to their hushed conversation.

"Daniel, you need to be extra careful with her. Who we are, what our real purpose is here, needs to remain a secret. Especially from her," said Eli.

"I know. You really think I need to be reminded of how important it is to keep our secret?" Daniel fidgeted in agitation. "Why would you think that I would suddenly slip up, especially now?"

"Look, I don't know, Danny. I just can see how you are with her. I get the feeling that you like her."

"What's not to like? Lily likes her, too. Heck, even you like her."

"Fine. Fair enough. But that's not what I'm talking about." Eli shook his head in frustration, sending his blond hair tumbling around his head. "You know who she really is. And you know how dangerous that information can be. I just don't want you to get too attached to her, that's all. Take it from me, Danny, if you let down your guard and forget your real mission, even for one second, someone could get hurt. Or worse."

"That's not going to happen, Eli," Daniel insisted. "Trust me. I've got this under control."

"I hope you're right. But you and I both know that if this goes down wrong, a lot of people are going to get hurt. A lot." Eli took a deep breath. "Just be extra careful with her. That's all I'm saying."

I staggered back a few steps, breathing heavily and shaking from head to toe. It was obvious that I was never supposed to hear that conversation. It was also obvious that I wasn't the only one at Provenance High keeping secrets.

CHAPTER FOUR

"I'm not sure you could've picked a nerdier way for us to spend our Sunday," Bax said as he watched me add yet another book to the stack nestled in my arms.

"You didn't have to come." I nudged him aside and reached for a copy of *The Road*.

"Put it down. That was a super depressing movie." Baxter grabbed the book and tossed it back on the shelf. "And yes, I did have to come. It was this or church with my Nana."

"I thought you liked your Nana?" I tried to remember if I already owned *This Side of Paradise*.

"Liking Nana isn't really the issue. Are we done here yet?" Bax sighed dramatically. "I'm ready to go shopping for some new shoes."

"You are such a girl sometimes," I said. "I just want to check the mythology section and then we can go pick out some new heels for you."

"Funny. Fine, I'm going to check the graphic novel section. Come find me when you are done being an uber-nerd."

"You're going to the graphic novel section and *I* am the uber-nerd?" I teased. Baxter just stuck out his tongue and I laughed.

I found the mythology section at the back of the store. It was surprisingly well-stocked for such a small bookstore. Some of the books were bound in old leather with intricate designs carved on their covers. I flipped through them, but they were written in languages I couldn't begin to understand. The books I was holding were starting to get heavy, so I gave up my hunt for the perfect book on Greek gods and tracked down Baxter.

"Finally. Shoe time?" Bax tossed away the magazine he had been pretending to read.

"Almost. Just let me pay for these." I dumped the books on the counter and waited for the man at the register to acknowledge me. When he finally looked up from the crossword puzzle that had been consuming his attention, he stared at me with narrowed eyes.

"Hello," I said, pushing the books closer to the register.

The man said nothing as he scanned the first book. He worked without looking away from me and I began to wonder if I had something on my face.

"Are you by chance hiring?" I asked. When I had mentioned to Daniel that I might be interested in a part-time job after school, he had told me about the bookstore where his sister worked. I was a big book nut, so mixing pleasure with business seemed like a good idea.

"I am," was the only response from the man with the unblinking eyes.

"I would be interested in applying. If that's okay with you." I handed the man some money to pay for the books and noticed that my hand was trembling.

"Fine. Be here tomorrow at 3:30. Don't be late." The man handed over my purchases.

"Tomorrow? Like for an interview?" I asked.

"For a job."

I croaked out a startled reply, "Okay." I heard Bax snicker and stepped hard on his foot as I turned away from the register. After a second, I turned back to the man. "What's your name, sir?"

"Bennett." Again, the unblinking stare.

"Bennett. Nice to meet you. I'm A-, Ally. My name is Ally." I almost smacked myself on the forehead. How was I going to pull off my new identity when I could barely offer the right name to someone who hadn't even asked for it? I followed Baxter to his car with a frown on my face.

"Congrats, Ally, you just got offered the worst job ever. Working for the creepiest boss ever. Sweet." Baxter opened the passenger door for me.

"Do you want me to go shoe shopping with you or

not?" I was just glad he hadn't seemed to notice my name stutter with Bennett.

"Shoe shopping alone is just sad. I promise to be good." Baxter held up his hand for a pinky swear.

"Let's not carried away," I joked.

Three pairs of shoes later, I collapsed on my bed. I had been battling an especially fierce headache for the last hour and now all I wanted to do was lay in a dark room until it passed. I remembered seeing some pain killers in the bathroom medicine cabinet and I attempted to stumble down the hall. Halfway there, I doubled over in pain and my vision went black.

It wasn't the first time I had been rendered immobile by a headache, so I knew there was nothing to do but crumble to the floor and wait for the moment to pass. Bright lights flashed inside my eyelids like mini lightning bolts. My ears filled with a rushing noise that blocked out all other sound.

It was over in less than five minutes, but it was enough to drain my energy. I crawled to the bathroom and grabbed the pills which I swallowed down with a mouthful of water from the tap. I barely made it back to my bed before the exhaustion overwhelmed me and I fell into a deep sleep.

I didn't wake up until the next morning. My family

was more than familiar with my headaches, so they knew the best thing they could do when one overtook me was to let me sleep it off. I had learned to accept the debilitating headaches as part of my life, but the increasing frequency of them was beginning to scare me. I had visited a specialist in New York who had run some tests and blamed it on stress. It was better than a serious diagnosis, but that made them almost impossible to treat.

The twelve hours of sleep had helped– the pain was gone. I was still physically weak from the toll it took on my body and I was still feeling out of sorts in homeroom. I even forgot to respond when the teacher called my name for attendance. Daniel had to reach over and poke me in the arm.

"Thanks," I said when the roll call was complete. "I'm a little out of it today."

"A little? You aren't even wearing shoes." Daniel looked at where my feet were resting under the desk.

"What?" I glanced down in horror and then let out an angry breath. "Not funny, Daniel."

"Actually, it was funny. You just didn't notice because you're too busy being stressed out." Daniel was teasing me, but he also looked concerned. "Trouble sleeping?"

"Nope, that was not a problem," I said, thinking of the hours of sleep I'd just experienced. "Migraine."

"That sucks. Do you get them a lot?"

"I used to get one every five or six months, but lately it's more like every month." I couldn't remember a time before the headaches, but I distinctly remembered them happening after my mom died. "It's not a big deal. They come, and then they go. When I'm stressed out, they come more often."

Daniel nodded and looked at me thoughtfully. "You need to take care of yourself. Don't let life stress you out so much. In fact, we should do something fun after school."

"Fun in Provenance? Interesting offer, but I can't today."

"Wow, you didn't even bother to let me down gently," Daniel said, putting an offended hand over his heart.

I rolled my eyes. "I got a job yesterday at that bookstore you told me about. The owner wants me to start today."

"Well, aren't you busy and important. Working woman taking on the world." Daniel's voice was strained and now it was my turn to be concerned.

I had been blocking out the conversation I had overheard at the party mostly because I didn't want to accept that Daniel was anyone other than who I had met the first day of school. There was no denying that he had a mysterious side to him, though, and that scared me. My life was frightening enough, and I didn't need to add any fuel to that fire.

I kept my distance from Daniel the rest of the day, which wasn't easy considering all the classes we shared. It helped that Baxter insisted on being my tennis doubles partner in gym class. I found myself regretting our partnership when his serve smacked me in the back of the head, but at least I could stop worrying about Daniel's secret for a while.

I was nervous when I walked into Bennett's Bookstore just before 3:30. Bennett was at the counter making notes on a ledger while a petite girl lectured him about the importance of keeping the best sellers stocked. I recognized the girl as Daniel's younger sister, Lily, from when I met her at the party.

"I know you love those educational books no one else has ever heard of, but if you want to draw people in, you have to keep up with what's hot."

"Excuse me," I said.

"Ally!" Lily greeted me like we were old friends. "I hear we are going to be working together. Are you super excited for all the fun awaiting you?"

"Work is not supposed to be fun. That's why it's

called work," Bennett said without looking up from his paperwork.

Lily winked at me. "Sure, Bennett. We promise not to have any fun at all tonight. Work, work, work."

"I will believe that when I see it." Bennett slid the ledger into a drawer and grabbed a tattered briefcase from the floor. "Please, train the new girl and try not to burn the place down."

"Aye, aye, Captain." Lily saluted grandly and Bennett shook his head.

"Teenagers," he mumbled as the door chimed on his way out.

"He seems friendly." I watched through the glass door as Bennett marched across the parking lot to beat up Chevy.

"He's old and crabby, but he's not a bad boss." Lily pulled herself up onto the counter and her butt knocked over a stack of books. "He'll warm up to you. Well, that might be exaggerating. But he won't give you a hard time."

"How long have you been working here?" I marveled at how comfortable and relaxed Lily seemed, her feet swinging lazily from her perch.

"A couple of weeks. We've only been in town a month." Lily jumped to the ground. "Shall we begin training?"

It took exactly twenty minutes for me to learn everything I needed to know about manning the bookstore. We spent the next four hours until closing time talking and pretending to shelve books. Lily had an infectious personality that was equal parts inviting and reserved. In that way, and that way alone, she was almost exactly like Daniel.

"So, tell me about your family," I said as matter-of-factly as possible. "It must be interesting having two older brothers."

"Not really." Lily's laugh was breathy. "It's more annoying than anything else. Boys are loud and dirty. Sometimes I think I'd trade both of them for one sister."

"Trust me, you are getting the better deal. Sisters are catty and jealous." I thought about all the silly fights Madelyn and I had growing up.

"The grass is always greener, I guess." Lily frowned at a copy of *Jane Eyre*. "Elliot isn't really my brother, you know."

I nearly dropped the pile of books I had been balancing in my hand. "He's not?"

"No. My parents, Gale and Eve, are really my foster parents. They took in me and Daniel when we were just kids. Elliot didn't come along until a few years ago." Lily glanced at me with a flick of her eyes.

I had no idea what to say. "Your parents sound like very special people."

"They are." Lily smiled. "Some kids who are adopted just want to find their biological parents but Daniel and I love our family. It doesn't matter to us where we came from because this is where we belong. I know that sounds cheesy." Her smile turned sheepish.

"No. It doesn't." I understood how Lily felt more than I could ever let her know. Maybe my life had taken some strange turns, but it almost felt like this was exactly where that road was supposed to lead.

"We should lock up." Lily took the rest of my books and tossed them on the counter. "We've worked hard enough for one day."

We said goodnight when we reached our cars and I couldn't stop thinking about our conversation. I was distracted as I turned the key in the ignition and almost didn't see the dark figure staring at me from across the parking lot. He was nearly hidden in the shadows, but I could just make out the glint of his eyes as he watched me.

If I hadn't been leading a secret life on the run, I probably would've just assumed he was some creepy guy. But my life wasn't that simple anymore. Not only that, but his eyes were so large and bright they didn't look human. I shook my head and told myself that I was being paranoid again, but something in the pit of my stomach told me this wasn't just a random encounter. I was being watched.

CHAPTER FIVE

"I can't believe they broke up," Cadence said in a hushed tone. "I mean, they were so perfect together."

"How would you know? You've never even met them." Baxter neglected to lower his voice and was immediately hushed by the librarian. I was using the lunch hour to research my English paper while Cadence was surfing the internet to find out about the latest celebrity breakups and Baxter was trying unsuccessfully to access adult sites.

"Quiet, you." Cadence tapped the mouse loudly and opened her email.

I felt a sudden urge to check my own email. Not the email that I had been using since arriving in Provenance, which almost certainly contained nothing but spam. I wanted to check my Alex Garretty email. As much as I had grown to love Cadence and Bax, I still missed my old friends terribly.

I knew it would be wrong and that it could create dangerous consequences. The problem was, I didn't really believe it. It seemed too ludicrous, too completely impossible, to be true. Just one quick look, that's all I needed.

I waited until I was sure Cadence and Baxter were preoccupied with their own computers and then quickly typed in my old email address and password. As soon as the screen lit up with my inbox, I regretted what I had done. How could I have been so careless? What if someone was watching this very account waiting for me to login and now they were tracking my location? How could I ever explain it to my father? And then I saw his name–Josh.

The subject line of his email was simple and heart-breaking. "Do you hate me?" I didn't want to open it, but I couldn't stop my finger from clicking the mouse. His words were brief, but that didn't make them any easier to read.

> *"Alex, it's been a month and I still haven't heard from you. I don't know what I did that made you never want to speak with me again, but I'm sorry. Please just reply so I know you are okay and I can stop harassing you. Love, Josh."*

When I switched back to my inbox, I saw at least two dozen more emails from Josh waiting to be read. I scanned the list until I found the first one.

> *"Alex, what's going on? You haven't been in school. You aren't answering your phone or responding to texts. Annabeth and Chloe haven't heard from you either. I even*

swung past your building and the doorman said your family
moved out in the middle of the night. I'm really starting to
worry-"

"Who's Josh?" Daniel said as he rolled a chair up next to me and took a seat. I jumped and clicked furiously on the mouse until the email disappeared. Cadence and Baxter both looked at me questioningly.

"Geez, Daniel. Way to sneak up on me. Don't you know it's rude to snoop on other people's private communications?" I could feel my heart pounding in my chest. It was bad enough that I had done exactly what I had been told not to do, but now I had also been caught in the act.

"Chill out. I wasn't snooping. You were just so engrossed I couldn't help but check out what you were reading." Daniel tapped the stack of papers next to the computer with his finger. "I just wanted to borrow your English notes. But we can discuss it later if you're too busy emailing your boyfriend."

I rolled my eyes, but I could feel my cheeks flush. "Take the notes, Stevens. Just don't lose them."

Daniel looked like he wanted to ask me something but thought better of it. He grabbed the notes slowly and I suddenly felt the need to say something that would make him stay a little while longer. In the past few days, I had been trying my best to avoid him and trying even more to forget his conversation with Eli. But the more I stayed away from him, the more I wanted to be around him.

"Are you going to Avenue Blue on Friday?" I said, turning back to my computer and opening the blank document that was supposed to be my paper. Baxter had convinced me and Cadence to come see him play with his band at a local dive that didn't check IDs. According to Bax, everyone who was anyone would be at Avenue Blue.

"Is this your subtle way of asking me on a date? Because I'm flattered, really, but I'm not into pushy girls."

"You are so annoying sometimes." I flipped my hair over my shoulder. "I was not asking you to go out with me. I was just asking if you were going."

"You need to learn how to take a joke, Ally," Daniel said, tapping my arm with the rolled-up notes in his hand. "What's happening at Avenue Blue Friday night?"

"Um, only the greatest band in Iowa happens to be playing," Baxter interjected. "It's kind of a big deal."

"Bax is in a band," I said with a smile.

"You don't say? Well, I don't see how I can possibly miss that. I guess I know where I'm going to be Friday night." Daniel returned my smile as he stood up. "Thanks for the notes."

"I think I may be starting to almost like that guy,"

Baxter said when Daniel was out of earshot.

"That's sweet. I think you should tell him that on Friday," I teased. "Oh! You could dedicate a song to him."

"Stop speaking nonsense, woman. Wretched Desires doesn't perform the kind of songs you dedicate to people you like." Baxter shook his head and let out an exasperated sigh. "We play the kind of songs you dedicate to people you despise."

The very fact that Avenue Blue had booked a band called Wretched Desires should've tipped me off that I was in over my head. The building was situated on the edge of town in an old warehouse. Inside it was just one big room with rafted ceilings. The bar took up the middle of the room with the stage along the wall opposite the door.

"This is... fun?" Cadence said, taking in the ambience. Directly in front of us was a shirtless man covered in tattoos up to his ears.

"Should we try to move closer to the stage?" I stood on my tiptoes, but I couldn't see much. "Should we be worried about how easy it was to get in?"

"Nah. This place lets in anyone with five dollars. As you can see, it's a classy establishment." Cadence gestured to a young girl in a short skirt that had just fallen off her chair. "Let's try to make it to the stage. Bax will never forgive us if we aren't standing front and center like worshipping groupies."

"What are the odds that Bax's band is any good?" I stepped out of the way just in time to avoid getting a beer spilled all over my shoes.

"Actually, they've had a couple of other gigs and they didn't sound too bad. It's not exactly my kind of music though, so it's hard for me to assess their actual skill level." Cadence waved at a group of girls that I vaguely remembered seeing at school.

Baxter took the stage with the band, all of them dressed in head to toe black. Baxter was the only one wearing any color- a red belt with a giant silver buckle. He smiled when he saw us and we both made a big deal about screaming his name. Baxter was the lead singer and when he grabbed the microphone and introduced the band, I almost couldn't believe he was the same goofy Bax that liked to go shoe shopping.

The music was a derivation of punk rock, loud and fast but not too heavy. The crowd was into it immediately and I was surprised to see many of them were singing along. Bax had *fans*. Cadence and I joined in, bouncing and swaying along with the rhythm of the crowd. Wretched Desires played five straight songs before taking a fifteen-minute break. The crowd groaned good-naturedly and dispersed to find drinks, hit the bathroom, and mingle.

"I can't believe it," Cadence said as she used her shirt sleeve to wipe the sweat from her forehead. "He actually came."

"Who?" I spun toward the door and spotted Daniel over the crowd. He looked completely unfazed by the drunken crowd that surrounded him. I turned back to Cadence. "I should go say hi."

"Yes, you should. I'm going to stand in line at the bathroom. See you in about an hour." Cadence took her place at the back of the line while I pushed my way through the crowd. I found Daniel near the bar looking attractively disinterested.

"You missed the first set," I said, watching as his face relaxed into a smile.

"I wouldn't say I missed it, I just wasn't here to see it." Daniel's eyes twinkled even in the dim light of the bar.

"They are actually kind of good," I confessed. "But if you were so sure they were going to be bad, why did you bother coming at all?"

Daniel shrugged. "Because you said you would be here." He leaned over the bar and asked for two waters. I used that time to stare at him in shock. I just barely managed to recompose myself when he handed me the drink.

"How did you guess my drink?" I sipped the ice-cold water gratefully. It was cramped in the bar and the area near the stage had been particularly stuffy.

"You don't really strike me as a drinker." Daniel froze when a hand clamped down on his shoulder.

"What are you, her dad?" Eli said, sliding a wink at me. "Barkeep, get this lady a house special. And two more for her unworthy companions."

"Eli–" Daniel's jaw was clenched and I jumped in to ease the tension.

"What's the house special?"

"It's cherry soda with a kick." Eli slid a twenty on the bar and handed me the drink.

Daniel was still annoyed, but his lips twitched as he fought a smile. "The kick being whiskey."

Daniel had been right– I wasn't a drinker. But I also didn't want to make a big deal over one drink, so I took a hesitant sip and fought off a wince as it burned on the way down.

"I'm supposed to meet Cade by the stage. Coming?" I wasn't sure I wanted Cadence to see me drinking, but I didn't really have a choice. I took another sip and plunged into the crowd.

"I ran into Bax and he says we aren't acting groupie enough, whatever that means," Cadence said when I found her in front of the stage. "Hey, Daniel."

Daniel nodded and said, "This is my brother, Eli. This is Cadence."

"It's a pleasure to meet you, Cadence," Eli said as he shook Cadence's hand. His lips pulled back in a charming smile. I coughed uncomfortably, but Cadence just giggled and ducked her head.

"The band is starting. Thank you, Bax," I muttered into my drink. Cadence stared suspiciously at my drink, but didn't say anything.

The music started up loud and fast and the crowd was back into it immediately, but I felt self-conscious standing between Daniel and Eli. I tried to focus on Baxter and the song, but my nerves got the best of me and I ended up finishing my drink without even meaning to.

Eli must have gone back to the bar because a few minutes later he was handing me another drink and I took it gratefully. I knew even as I was finishing that second drink that it was a bad idea. I was smarter than that. But for the first time in two months, I felt myself relaxing and it felt great.

It wasn't until halfway through my third drink that I realized I had gone too far. I was having trouble standing up straight and Daniel had to reach out to steady me more than once. Eli seemed to be enjoying the show and even offered to get me another drink until he saw Daniel's reaction.

"Let's get some fresh air," Daniel yelled into my ear when I stumbled into him for the third time. I was helpless to protest and let him pull me outside. Cadence started to follow us, but Eli assured her that Daniel would handle it.

"It feels good out here," I said, tilting back my head to let the breeze cool my face. My hair was sticking to the sweat on the back of my neck and I used my hands to lift it away from my skin. Daniel led me around the building and sat me on a concrete bench. Standing over me, he looked even taller and more imposing than usual.

"Sit down. You're making me nervous." I leaned over and rested my head in my hands. Everything was starting spin and it was making me sick to my stomach.

"You drank too much," Daniel finally said. He sat next to me, but kept his distance.

"Wow, you don't miss anything," I snapped.

"So, you're an angry drunk."

"I'm not a drunk, but you're a jerk." I could hear myself sounding like a child, but I couldn't seem to stop. "You should be more like Eli."

"Eli? You think I should be more like my brother?" Daniel laughed in disbelief.

I fixed him with my harshest glare. "Eli's not your

brother."

Daniel froze and a guarded look passed over his face. "How do you know that?"

"Your sister told me. You should be more like her, too. She's nice." I wondered if I would be able to walk away without falling over and decided to stay put.

"She shouldn't have told you that." Daniel sounded almost sad and I felt a little guilty for being so mean.

"It's not a big deal. I haven't told you the truth about me either. We all have secrets." I wondered if I had said too much, but then another wave of nausea crashed in my stomach.

"What secrets could you possibly be keeping, Ally?" Daniel was speaking very quietly now and I lowered my voice, too.

"My name isn't really Ally." I snapped a hand over my mouth and laughed. "And I'm not from St. Louis!"

"Maybe we should go back inside and get you some water," Daniel suggested, looking worried as a couple of kids from school rounded the corner.

"That's not all. My sister's real name is Madelyn. And I have a boyfriend named Josh who is waiting for me back in New York." Daniel grabbed my arm and hauled me to my feet. I was unsteady and leaned against him as we walked. "Also, I know you aren't who you say you are either. I know you have a secret."

Daniel's steps faltered and he almost lost his grip on me. He shifted his hold and pulled me closer to keep from dropping me. I was close enough to see the worry lines around his eyes and tightness of his lips. I was also close enough to fully appreciate his good looks. "You have nice eyes," I whispered and he gave me a surprised smile.

"So do you," he said. "Now pull yourself together so they don't kick you out for being drunk."

I took a couple of deep breaths and stood up straighter. I still had to lean on Daniel to steady myself, but at least I wasn't tripping over my own feet anymore. The doorman barely even looked at us and Daniel went straight to the bar and got me a large glass of water.

"Sit and drink," he said as he placed me on a barstool.

"Bax is going to be mad we missed the end of the show," I said between drinks. The stage was empty and the crowd had thinned. I wondered if Cadence was still around or if I was going to have to find a ride home from someone else.

"What happened to you guys?" Eli said as he slammed an empty glass on the bar. "Things were just getting good."

I didn't know if he was referring to the band or to my public display of drunkenness. "Things were getting a little spinny. I needed some air."

"That's too bad," Eli said leaning close. "Things got a lot less enjoyable once you were gone."

"Where the heck have you been?" Baxter said as he marched up to me with his arms thrown wide in an exasperated gesture.

"Bax!" I forgot about the spinning world and jumped to my feet. I could feel myself beginning to fall, so I launched myself at Baxter in a poor attempt at a hug. Bax laughed in surprise, but hugged me back. "Your band is awesome and you are the best lead singer ever."

"Wow. You are drunk," he said, laughing again. "I think I like drunk you though."

"Don't encourage her," Daniel muttered.

"We should probably get you home, huh?" Baxter pulled away from my death grip and wrapped an arm around my waist to keep me upright. "Say goodbye to your friends."

"Goodbye, friends." I squinted at Eli. "Except we don't really know each other, so I don't think we're friends. But goodbye anyway."

"Goodbye, Alex. Don't worry, we're going to be excellent friends." Eli wasn't looking at me when he said it. He was looking at Daniel and Daniel was staring right back.

CHAPTER SIX

I was barely able to function the next day. My head was pounding and my stomach threatened to wage war at any moment. To make matters worse, I couldn't even sleep it off because I had some serious damage control to do.

I had made a huge mistake accepting Eli's drinks and letting my guard down. Because of that error in judgment, I had told Daniel too much information about my past. I had to talk to him and tell him the whole truth. It was the only hope I had of convincing him to keep my secret. He already knew at least a little of the truth and probably suspected more, but I didn't know how much. If I could tell him my side of everything, maybe I could persuade him to keep my secret.

After I had popped a couple of aspirin and spent thirty minutes in a scalding shower, I felt strong enough to face him. I sent him a text asking if we could meet up and then waited anxiously for the reply. It came almost immediately– clearly Daniel had some things he wanted to discuss as well. We agreed to meet at a small coffee joint aptly name The Coffee Shop. I suspected it would be almost empty this early on a Saturday and I was proven right when I walked in twenty minutes later.

Two elderly gentlemen were seated at a table near the front, so I ordered a latte and found a seat near the back. I kept worrying that Daniel would decide he had nothing to say to me, but three minutes later he arrived and ordered a large coffee before taking the seat across from me.

"She lives," he said as he settled into his seat.

"Hopefully," I muttered, thinking about all the rules I had broken in the past 24 hours.

Daniel's coffee was steaming and he blew on it softly before taking a sip. "So… you wanted to talk."

I couldn't think of a good way to broach the subject, so I just jumped right in. "I had a lot to drink last night and I told you some things I was never supposed to tell anyone."

I waited for Daniel to interrupt with a smart remark, but he just nodded. "Anyway, I think I need to tell you the full truth so you'll understand why you can't ever tell anyone what I told you."

"I wouldn't tell anyone," he said quietly. "We're friends, Ally."

"Are we? I mean we barely even know each other. And you don't even know the real me." I could feel myself getting frustrated and that was only going to make this even harder. "Daniel, this isn't the kind of secret friends keep and then laugh about in private. This is a matter of life and death."

"Okay, go ahead." Daniel didn't really seem surprised by my doomsday declaration.

"Two months ago, my name was Alex Garretty and I was living in Manhattan with my family. My father worked for the FBI and he got involved in some New York mob thing. The details aren't important, but he got in too deep and his life was in danger so my whole family had to move. They gave us new identities and brought us here." Just in case Daniel wasn't following, I added, "We're in the witness protection program, Daniel."

I wasn't sure what kind of response I had been expecting, but Daniel's complete lack of reaction caught me off guard. I had been expecting him to laugh or call me a liar. Maybe even express concern over my safety. Instead, he just leaned back in his chair and crossed his arms over his chest. "Huh."

"Huh? That's all you've got to say?" I was a little disappointed. Here I had been keeping this big secret for two months and now the only response I got was 'huh'.

"What do you want me to say?" Daniel looked thoroughly confused.

"Forget it." I took a deep breath and reached for my

latte. "Do you at least understand why you can't say anything to anyone?"

"I already wasn't going to say anything, but yes I get it. This doesn't really change anything though, Ally. You still want me to call you Ally, right?"

"Yes. That's super important. No one can know my real name or my entire family could be put at risk." I felt a rush of guilt realizing that what I had just told Daniel could have jeopardized my entire family's safety.

"Okay. Consider this whole thing forgotten. We can still be friends, right?" He was trying to be reassuring, but it was a wasted effort because even though I barely even knew him, I trusted Daniel.

Ever since my mother had died, I had found it almost impossible to trust anyone. I had built up a wall around me that no one could get past, not even my family. I felt safer keeping everyone out because if they couldn't get in then they couldn't hurt me. But Daniel was different. Somehow, he had never been on the other side of that wall. He had always been on the inside and that scared the crap out of me.

"Yeah, sure. Friends." I suddenly didn't feel well. I felt like I always did when I was about to get one of my headaches, except this time it was much more sudden. "I'll be right back. I just need to use the restroom."

I stumbled into the closet-like room and went directly to the sink. I cupped my hands and filled them with water before splashing my face. The water was cold and the shock of it snapped me back to reality. I took deep breaths, counting to ten until my head cleared. "Pull it together, Alex," I said to the frightened looking girl in the mirror.

As I headed back to the table, I approached Daniel from behind and noticed that he was on the phone. I was still far enough away that he didn't sense me approaching and I could just barely make out his voice.

"She doesn't know anything, Eli. They've been lying to her. They've told her just enough to put her in danger. She knows someone is after her, but she doesn't know why. And she doesn't have a clue about who she really is." Daniel's voice was so low I wondered if I was just imagining the words. But I sensed that what I was hearing was 100% real. Daniel was silent as he listened to whatever Eli was saying.

"It's not our place to tell her. She wouldn't believe us anyway. It will be best if she discovers it on her own." Daniel listened again and I could tell from the way he held his shoulders that he was getting angry. "This isn't your call, Eli. It's mine. Alex is my responsibility, not yours."

I felt like I had been punched in the stomach. Not

only was he discussing me with Eli, he was using my real name– a name I had only told him in confidence. I might have been honest with Daniel, but he had clearly lied to me.

"Have a nice chat with Eli?" I asked when he had hung up.

If he was surprised that I had overheard the conversation, he didn't let it show. "As nice as any chat with him can be. Listen, Ally, I've got to go. Eli just reminded me that I have somewhere to be."

I didn't say a word as Daniel got up to leave. In those two minutes that I had been away from the table, everything between us had changed. Daniel wouldn't look me in the eye and I couldn't think of anything to say to him.

"See ya around," was all Daniel said before leaving. I sat at the table long after he had left. Daniel and Eli knew more about me than they would admit, and apparently, they even knew something about me that I didn't know. Daniel clearly wasn't about to say anything, but I had other options if I wanted to get to the truth.

I was given the perfect opportunity the next day at work. Lily and I were in the storage room doing inventory and it was as good a time as any to pump her for information.

"Why did your family move to Provenance?" I asked as I marked a check on the list I was holding.

"Our foster dad got a good job offer." Lily didn't have any obvious tells, but I knew she was lying. She had the same guarded look that Daniel had when he wasn't being honest.

"Hmm that must've been a really nice job to pick up the whole family and move. And Eli even came with you guys. Isn't he a legal adult?" I realized I wasn't being very subtle, but Lily didn't seem to notice.

"He turned eighteen a few months ago. But he's our family, so it's not like we were going to leave him behind." Lily looked at me with suspicion. "What's with the interrogation?"

I tried to look nonchalant. "I'm just curious about your family. Daniel never really talks about himself. You don't have to answer me if you don't want to."

"I don't mind. There just isn't much to tell. We're pretty boring." Lily grabbed a water-logged copy of *East of Eden* and tossed it in a box with the rest of the damaged books. "You don't really talk about your family either, you know."

I only wished that was true. If I had kept my mouth shut, I wouldn't be in this predicament. If I could just find out what secret Eli and Daniel were keeping, I could use that to make Daniel keep his mouth shut about me. Mutual destruction or something.

"Eli seems interesting. He's very friendly." I pretended to check my paperwork for a book title.

Lily smiled knowingly. "Eli's a big flirt. But he's harmless. Mostly. But that doesn't mean I want any of my friends to date him, so stay away." She shook her finger at me.

"No worries there. He's not exactly my type." I remembered the leering looks he had given me and the way he leaned over me when he talked. He was intimidating, and I could stand to have less intimidation in my life.

"Good. But that won't necessarily stop him because you are definitely *his* type." Lily tossed her clipboard on the nearest shelf and plopped down on the floor. "I'm tired. Let's take a break."

I had failed at my mission of getting Lily to spill the beans, but I still had one more option. If Daniel wasn't talking, and Lily didn't have the information I needed, I was going to the source. I just had to figure out a way to meet up with Eli without Daniel finding out.

While I was on my break with Lily, I found out that Eli was attending the local college. All I had to do was stalk him on campus and I could confront him. But that meant ditching school which I'd never actually done. This was as good a time as any I figured.

I drove Madelyn to school on Monday like always, but halfway across the parking lot I claimed to have left something in my car. I waited until Madelyn was inside before starting up the car and pulling away. The college was located a few blocks away, as was everything in Provenance. I parked on the street a couple of blocks away and walked to the area called the Quad figuring a high traffic area was my best bet.

I grabbed a book from my book bag and pretended to read while sitting under a tree facing the main walking path. It was still early, so campus was pretty empty. It didn't start getting busy until a couple of hours later. I wanted to go find some coffee, but I was afraid I would miss Eli in those few minutes away. Not for the first time, I began to wonder if Lily had even been telling the truth about Eli being enrolled there.

"Are you stalking me?" someone asked from behind me. I knew it was Eli even before I turned around. He had walked across the open lawn rather than follow the paved path and it had led him directly to me and my tree.

"Stalking you? I didn't even know you went here." I tried to look insulted.

Eli smiled his smug smile that said he didn't believe

me. "Sure. So why are you here then?"

"My dad has been on my back to start thinking about college. I figured I might as well start local." It was the best lie I could come up with and Eli saw right through it.

"Shouldn't you have signed up for one of the campus tours? And I don't think your dad would be too happy about you skipping school." Eli wasn't the type of person to just let it go and I didn't have time to waste.

"Fine. I did come to see you. I need to talk to you." I ignored the cocky look Eli gave me. "Is there someplace private we can talk?"

"Naturally. The ladies can't resist me. You drink coffee?" Eli shifted the messenger bag slung over his shoulder and looked around to see if anyone was listening to our conversation. I agreed to his coffee suggestion and he led me to the small campus café. It was crowded inside, but after he bought us each a large coffee he led me to a quiet table out back.

"So, what can I do for you, Alex?" he asked in a bored voice.

"We can start with that. You know my real name." I appreciated that Eli didn't seem to shy from the truth.

"I do. I know a lot of other things about you, too." Eli leaned his elbows on the table. "What do you know about me?"

"Not much. Lily told me you aren't her real brother. She also told me you are a womanizer and I should stay away from you." I couldn't help but enjoy the annoyed flicker in his eyes.

"Lily has a big mouth. Did she tell you why we moved to Provenance?"

"She said her foster dad got a job offer."

"But you didn't believe her?" Eli glanced up as a girl walked by in tight jeans and his eyes followed her progress.

"I didn't believe her about the job, no. About you being a womanizer, yes." I bunched up a napkin and tossed it at Eli's face.

Eli turned back to me with a guilty smile. "What if I told you we moved here because of you? Would that surprise you?"

"Nothing surprises me anymore." The notion of them moving because of me seemed ridiculous, but it didn't surprise me.

"I take it Daniel doesn't know you are here." Eli's lip twitched ever so slightly when he said Daniel's name.

"Are you changing the subject?"

"No, but it's not my place to answer your questions. You need to ask Daniel." Eli finished off his coffee and glanced at his watch.

"That's it then? Just like that you are done talking to

me?" I was disappointed. I had really thought that Eli would open up to me without Daniel around. He was arrogant and a know-it-all, the perfect combination for having a big mouth.

"Daniel may not be my real brother, but he's still my family and my best friend. He wouldn't approve of us meeting like this, and I have to respect his wishes." Eli stood up, effectively ending our conversation. "I have to get to class, but let me walk you to your car."

"How noble of you." I hated that when I stood next to him, he towered over me like I was a child. "I gather this is your way of making sure I actually leave?"

"Let's go." Eli placed his hand on the small of my back and guided me across the lawn. I noticed that some of the girls we passed gave us dirty looks and I wondered how many of them were Eli's conquests.

"You've made a lot of friends," I said after one girl actually swore at us.

"People tend to have strong opinions about me." Again, he offered me a cocky smile. "Especially women."

"I can't imagine why." I wondered how Daniel could be friends with someone like Eli. "Does Daniel approve of you being such a jerk?"

"Daniel has a pretty high tolerance for flawed human beings. Which explains his friendship with you." Eli was walking slightly ahead of me now, so I couldn't see what caused Eli to flinch. "I suspect that friendship may be about to hit a speed bump."

"What are you talking–" I pulled ahead of Eli and found Daniel leaning against my car. His arms were crossed and he looked more annoyed than I would've thought was possible.

"What are you doing here?" I said without thinking.

Daniel's eyes were fixed on Eli when he spoke to me. "I could ask you the same thing."

"I mean it, Daniel. Why are you here? You aren't in charge of me." I was tired of not having control over my own life. I was tired of people telling me where I could and couldn't go and who I could and couldn't see.

"She has a point, Danny," Eli said. I wished he would just keep his mouth shut. "But don't worry. She was just leaving. You two should talk." He gave Daniel a pointed look that wasn't lost on me. He had told me to ask Daniel directly, and now he was giving me the chance.

"Later, kids. See you at home, Danny." Eli sauntered away with his hands tucked into his pockets.

"What a jerk." I said out loud with realizing it.

Daniel laughed. "He takes some getting used to. But he's one of the good guys."

"And you?"

Daniel shrugged. "It remains to be seen. Did you two have a nice chat?"

"Not really, no." I frowned when I thought about what Eli had said about Daniel's family moving to Provenance because of me. "How did you know where to find me?"

"When you didn't show up at school I asked around. Bax and Cadence figured you must be sick. And Lily may have mentioned the talk you two had about Eli. It wasn't hard to guess from there." Daniel scuffed his foot at the ground. "Did you learn anything interesting?"

"You moved here because of me?" I wanted to see if Daniel could give me a straight answer for once.

"More or less. But it could also be said that you moved here because of me."

"That doesn't make any sense." I wanted to scream or punch something. All I wanted was the truth, and all I kept getting was a bunch of cryptic responses. "How are we connected? How do you and Eli know all these things about me that no one else knows?"

Daniel pushed off from the car and stepped closer to me. For just a moment, his guard dropped and he looked like he was going to answer all my questions. I found myself stepping closer to him and then the wall went back up. "I can't answer that."

"Of course, you can't." I shook my head in frustration. "Remember when I told you my big secret and you asked if we could still be friends?"

Daniel nodded.

"Well friendships work two ways. If you can't be honest with me, then I don't want you as a friend." I felt terrible as soon as the words left my mouth, but I also meant it. I couldn't trust someone that wasn't honest with me and I couldn't be friends with someone I didn't trust.

"Alex, I'm only trying to protect you. I don't know what else to do." Daniel sounded broken and vulnerable. I nearly caved at hearing my real name. I wanted to just be able to blindly trust that Daniel was looking out for me, but that kind of faith just wasn't in my DNA.

I stopped next to the car door and gave him one last chance to change his mind. When he said nothing, I yanked the door open. "Goodbye, Daniel."

CHAPTER SEVEN

I ended up going to school after all. I told Ms. Copeland that my car had broken down and I'd had to wait for a tow truck. I felt a little bad when the secretary made a big fuss and wrote me a late slip. The same excuse worked on Baxter and Cadence and I worried that I might be getting too comfortable with lying.

"Is it just me, or is Daniel acting weirder than usual?" Baxter said while bouncing a rubber ball next to me in the center of the gym. Mr. T was even less thrilled about his job than usual and had given a vague command for us to "play some dodgeball."

The students had gathered on the gym floor in a few different circles. One group was actually making a rather vicious attempt at the game, but most of the others had broken off into groups of friends chatting amongst themselves. Daniel had returned to school later in the day as well, but he hadn't even looked in my direction.

"He's a weird guy. Why do you care?" I knew I was being defensive, but I still felt bad about the way things had ended between us. I wasn't exactly in a position to be turning down friends.

"I thought you two were buds." Baxter bounced the

ball off my forehead and waggled his eyebrows. "Or maybe something more?"

"Grow up." I swatted Bax in the arm. He was just being his usual obnoxious self, but I had to wonder if he was right. Not in the way he meant, of course, but it was clear Daniel and I had some sort of connection that had caused us both to end up in Provenance.

"Bax. Do you think there's something, I don't know, off about me?" I needed an outsider's opinion on the matter.

"Huh?" Baxter stopped dribbling the ball and appraised me. "Well, you're kind of tall for a girl. And you have weird taste in music."

"Be serious, Bax," I said even though I wasn't sure it was possible for Baxter to be serious. "Do I give off a weird vibe or something?"

"I guess you are a little mysterious. I mean, I'm pretty much your best friend in the whole world and I don't know anything about you. Other than your crappy taste in music."

"My musical taste is fine. Just because I hadn't heard of your band until I moved here doesn't mean I'm musically deprived." I appreciated that Baxter was trying to keep things light. "I'm not mysterious. I just lead a really boring life that isn't worth talking about."

"If you say so. Look, don't shoot the messenger. You asked me what I thought, and that's what I think. But otherwise, you're pretty okay." Baxter gave me a hopeful smile. "Are we done with this line of questioning?"

"Sure, Bax. Thanks for your honesty." I turned away from him and my eyes immediately landed on Daniel. He was across the gym, but he was watching me like he had heard every word. His face was pained and I fought the urge to go to him. I need some distance to figure things out. That would be easier if I didn't have almost every class with him.

The next couple of weeks were more of the same. Daniel and I didn't speak, but I would catch him watching me. I hated that I couldn't talk to Cadence or Baxter about it because that would mean telling them what our fight had been about. Even surrounded by my friends I felt completely alone.

It wasn't much of a surprise when I found myself reading Josh's emails again. At least this time I didn't have to worry about Daniel lurking over my shoulder. The emails got progressively harder to read. Josh was confused at first, then angry. I didn't blame him. My sudden departure hadn't just affected me, it had affected everyone in my life and Josh had been a huge part of my life.

I couldn't explain why I did it. I could blame it on

being lonely or being confused about my fight with Daniel. I could blame it on the pressure of starting a new life or the stress of assuming a new identity. But none of that was the real reason I decided to reply to Josh. The real reason was quite simple– I missed him.

My response was brief. I told him that I was okay and that I was sorry I had left without saying goodbye. I explained that it had to be that way, and that it was out of my control. I told him that I missed him and I hoped I would see him again someday, but I didn't think it was likely. When I was done, I hit send on the email before I could talk myself out of it.

I should have felt guilty about breaking the number one rule. I should have been worried about the potential repercussions. Instead, I just felt sad. My life was seriously messed up right now and I had no idea how to fix it.

I had another bad headache that night. This time, I made it to my bed before my head exploded in bright lights and the roaring noise overtook me. Instead of the normal blinding pain, this time I caught the faintest image of a man. The man looked normal, but not at all familiar. He came more into focus and I could see that the whites of his eyes were a shade of burning gold that flashed with heat. He pulled back his lips and bared two rows of pointed fangs.

When the vision cleared, I tried to convince myself that I had fallen asleep and had a crazy dream. It was better than accepting the truth– that I was having visions about monsters. I took some solace in the fact that this headache hadn't lasted as long as the others. Less time spent writhing in pain was always a good thing in my book.

"Somewhere to be?" I asked Lily the next day at work. Lily had been checking the time on her phone every five minutes for the last hour.

"Actually, yes. We are having this thing for the cheer squad. We're supposed to go decorate the gym for the pep rally tomorrow." Lily gave me a sheepish look. "I wouldn't just abandon you though."

I laughed at Lily's lack of subtlety. "Go. Get out of here. I can close up by myself tonight."

"You're sure?" Lily was already halfway to the door. "I will so totally owe you one."

"I'm sure. Go. Have fun." I watched Lily skip out the door and wished I had one tenth of her energy.

Closing the bookstore was a relatively painless activity. I locked the front door and emptied the cash register. After counting the money and recording it in the ledger, I locked it up in the safe in the storage room. Then I flipped the sign in the door to "Closed" and stepped outside. The door had two deadbolts that clicked into place as I locked them. The key got stuck in the second lock and I was so focused on getting it out without breaking it off in the lock that I didn't feel the man approach me from behind.

He shoved me up against the door, smacking my head against the glass. The force of it sent stars dancing across my vision. I could feel his breath on the back of my neck.

"A pretty little thing like you shouldn't be alone at night," he said, his voice dripping with venom. I was convinced in that instant that the men my family had been running from had found me. I knew I was going to die, and it was probably all my fault for reaching out to Josh. But then the man said something that made no sense.

"I expected more of a fight. You aren't a very good Warrior standing here all helpless. It's going to take a lot of the fun out of killing you." He turned me around, presumably so that he could look into my eyes when he killed me, and that's when I realized he was the man from my dream.

A deeper look confirmed he wasn't a man at all. His eyes were even more inhuman in person and the sharp points of his fangs looked deadly. I winced as I pictured the fangs piercing my skin.

"Not even a snappy comeback? I'm so disappointed."

The sight of those fangs laughing made me turn my head away and when I did, I saw Daniel standing less than ten feet away. He was perfectly still and utterly silent. My first thought was to call out to him, but then I realized he wasn't going to help me. He was there to watch.

My attacker had grown tired of trying to get a reaction out of me. I felt those fangs getting closer, but I didn't try to stop it. I was still in shock from seeing Daniel and I was angry at myself for ever trusting him. That anger came in handy when the monster moved in for the kill. I dodged to the left and brought up my knee just in time to catch him in the gut.

He reared back and let out a growl. I froze, not sure what to do next. I wanted to run, but he was blocking my path. I backed up until I felt the door against my back.

"Alex!" Daniel called calmly. I turned my head just in time to catch the object he tossed in my direction. When my hand closed around it, I realized it was a metal dagger. I turned it in my hand as the monster dove at me and I managed to drive it into his chest just as his body crashed into mine.

We slammed into the door and then fell to the ground with the monster's body trapping me. He was no longer moving, but he was heavy and the weight of his body was making it hard for me to breathe. Daniel hefted the body away and kneeled over me.

"You alright?" He didn't look particularly concerned.

"That man… or whatever he was. Is he dead?" I sat up slowly and my body screamed in protest.

"Shadow. And yeah, he's dead." Daniel and I looked to where the body lay and that was when I saw the black liquid oozing from his mouth and ears.

"We need to call the police." I began to panic. Technically, I had just murdered someone.

"No need. The body will dissolve now that it no longer has a Soul or Shadow keeping it together." Daniel grabbed me by the arm and hauled me to my feet. He retrieved the dagger from where it was still imbedded in the body and when he pulled it out, it was covered in more of the black, sticky liquid.

"Daniel. What's going on?" I could feel that I was about to fall apart.

"We need to get inside. There could be more." Daniel glanced around the parking lot and pushed me toward the bookstore. The key was still stuck in the lock and he made quick work of unlocking the door. He relocked it behind us once we were inside.

Daniel moved me further inside, away from the windows at the front of the store. "Alex, are you okay? Say something?" He searched my eyes for some sign that I was okay.

"Daniel. What is going on?" My head was spinning with confusion and throbbed where it had been smacked against the glass. I wondered if the confusion was only because of the unbelievable series of events that just took place, or if perhaps I might have a concussion.

"You're bleeding," Daniel observed. "Come."

I stood firm. I wasn't going to let Daniel weasel his way out of answering my questions this time. "Answer me, Daniel!"

He looked at me in surprise. "Alex, I'm not avoiding the question, okay? I just want to check your wound and make sure you're alright. I promise, after that I will answer everything."

I followed him to the bathroom where he found a first aid kit under the sink and let him inspect my wound and clean it. He was surprisingly gentle and seemed to know what he was doing. I wondered how many wounds he had cleaned and dressed in his life. "It's already closing up. I don't think it will leave a scar," he said as he covered it with a band aid.

"Do you do this kind of thing often?" I touched the area around the wound and found it was only a little tender.

"Often enough." Daniel tossed the bloody gauze into

the toilet and flushed it.

"You let that thing attack me," I said.

"I did." Daniel leaned against the wall.

I had expected him to deny it, to tell me that I was crazy. I expected him to defend himself in some way, but he didn't seem at all bothered by admitting the truth.

"Why? Why did he attack me and why did you let him?" I wasn't angry, just completely lost. Nothing that had happened made sense.

Daniel took in a deep breath and exhaled slowly. "There's just so much you don't know. I don't even know where to start."

"You could try starting from the beginning. And don't leave anything out. I want to know whatever you know."

The look on Daniel's face was skeptical, but he said, "I'll try. I'm not sure we'll have enough time tonight to get through everything, but I'll do my best."

I settled against the edge of the sink and waited for him to begin. He seemed to be stuck on where to start, so I gave him some help. "I'm not normal, am I?"

"No."

"And you're not normal either?" I was sure of this.

"No. I'm more normal than you, but still a pretty big freak show." I noticed a complete lack of humor in his voice.

"Okay, so I'm a freak. Why? What's so different about me?"

"I don't really know how to answer that. However I say this, it's going to sound crazy," Daniel said.

I groaned. "Just spit it out. I already think you're crazy so get it over with."

"Fine. You're a Warrior."

"I'm sorry, I'm a what?" I couldn't possibly have heard him correctly.

"A Warrior. Well, technically a pre-Warrior because you won't become a full Warrior until you're 18." Daniel held up his hands as if to say I told you so and I was certain that he was certifiably crazy. Or that I had been knocked unconscious outside and this was all some delusional dream.

"A Warrior." I tried out the word. "Warrior. A Warrior of what? What am I supposed to fight?"

Daniel was surprised. "Demons, of course. Alex, you are a demon hunter."

CHAPTER EIGHT

I started laughing and once I started, I couldn't stop. I laughed so hard that I had tears in my eyes. "A demon hunter?" I gasped.

"It's actually not that funny." Daniel did smile a little bit though. "Or maybe it is funny if you don't believe me and think I'm completely insane."

"No, actually, it's funny because I think maybe I do believe you." I contemplated whether it was possible I had suffered brain damage when I banged my head. That would explain how I could be considering the truth of Daniel's proclamation. "Are you saying demons walk among us?"

"In a way. They aren't complete demons though, just demons possessing human bodies. We call them Shadows." Daniel yawned. "Sorry, it's been a long day."

"So that thing outside was a Shadow? A demon possessing a human?" I shivered. "No wonder he was so freaky looking."

"Shadows normally pass as regular humans. Their inner demon only shows itself when they are embracing their demon nature. Like attacking you."

"Let's say I believe you about these Shadows. It's a little hard to deny after having just stabbed one in the chest." I couldn't stop thinking about how it had felt to sink the dagger into his chest. "How did I get chosen to hunt these things?"

Daniel's phone rang just then and he checked the caller ID before hitting ignore. "No one really knows the answer to that. What we do know is there are dozens of Warriors like yourself around the world. Your job is to fight the Shadows and prevent them from destroying the barrier between Earth and hell."

"That sounds easy," I said sarcastically. "And what's your job in all this?"

"To protect you and to train you." Daniel pointed to the dagger lying on the sink, still covered in demon blood. "I'm a Guardian. There are hundreds of Guardians and we are assigned to a Warrior. We protect them until they turn 18. We train them, teach them what they need to know and set them free once their full powers have come in."

"You don't actually fight the Shadows? You have us do it for you?" I thought that was a load of crap.

Daniel seemed equally bothered by it. "We help fight the Shadows when it's needed, usually only before our assigned Warrior comes of age. We aren't blessed with the same skills and power as the Warriors."

"Skills and powers? I like the sound of that."

"Considering those skills and powers will likely get you killed, you may want to reconsider your excitement." Daniel's phone buzzed again, but he ignored it.

"Thanks for that, Sergeant Buzzkill. So, what else? What else do I need to know?" I was eager to learn everything I could from Daniel. If he was right and my life was in danger, I wanted to be prepared.

"You need to know more than I could possibly tell you tonight. You'll also need to meet with the Guardianship as soon as possible," he said with a visible grimace.

"The Guardianship?"

"It's a council of the highest-ranking Guardians. Generally, the members are spread around the world and they convene a couple of times each year. This time, they are meeting in Provenance and I have no doubt they will want to meet with you." Daniel moved toward the door, but I wasn't done asking questions.

"Why are they meeting here? And why did you and I end up here? What's so special about Provenance?" I would've kept going, but Daniel held up a hand to stop me.

"Alex, I promise we can talk about this more. But it's late and I need to get you home. We can talk as much as you want tomorrow. And the next day. But can we please call it a night?" Daniel looked and sounded tired. I, on the other hand, was brimming over with energy. Now that I finally knew the truth, I wanted to learn everything I could about my alleged calling.

"Okay. We'll talk tomorrow," I agreed reluctantly. Daniel stood lookout as I locked up the shop for the second time that night. I glanced to where we had left the body and found that Daniel had been right– it was gone. All that was left was a puddle of black goo that could easily be mistaken for oil from a leaky car.

"Where's your car?" I asked when I saw that my car was the only one in the lot.

"I walked."

"I'll give you a ride home," I offered.

"No. Drive us to your house. I'll walk home from there." Daniel made sure to check the backseat before he let me get in.

"That's crazy. You can't walk home. Let me drive you." I was feeling braver now that I was locked safely inside my car.

"It's non-negotiable." Daniel reached for the lever under the seat and pushed back. His long legs barely fit even with the seat as far back as possible. "Besides it's only about a mile walk. I'll be fine."

We were both quiet as I drove, neither of us quite sure how to act around the other now that all our secrets were laid bare. I was glad it was only a short drive to my house.

"We're here," I said as I pulled the car next to the curb. Dad's car was in the driveway and the light in his office was on. I realized that I was over an hour late getting home from work and I had forgotten to call. "Crap."

"Everything looks okay," Daniel said after he had surveyed the area. I headed toward the house, but stopped when I realized Daniel was following me.

"What are you doing?" I asked in alarm.

"I'm walking you to the door."

"Oh, no, you're not." I checked to make sure Dad wasn't watching from the window. "It's bad enough I'm showing up late, but it's only going to be worse if my dad sees me coming home with you."

"That's ridiculous. Parents love me." Daniel smiled and seemed to be feeling much more like himself. "Besides, I need to make sure you get there safely. If you think your dad wouldn't approve of me, I think he might not like it even more if you got slaughtered on his doorstep."

"You don't know my dad." Dad had only accepted

Josh a few weeks before we left town. "Anyway, you just said the coast was clear. I think I can make it these last few yards on my own."

"Yeah, alright." Daniel faded back to the sidewalk. "I'll just wait here until you get inside."

"Thanks," I said. "For everything, I guess."

We shared a moment of awkward silence and then I hurried up the driveway. I knew that I had some explaining to do once I went inside, but that wasn't the only reason I hesitated on the porch. I turned back and Daniel was still standing in the shadows, watching over me.

Between Daniel watching outside and my overbearing father waiting for me inside, I was suddenly feeling very safe which was odd considering that I had just almost been killed by a Shadow demon.

The next day, Dad left me in charge of Tommy while he went to work. I had been hoping to have the entire Saturday to talk to Daniel about the revelations of the previous night. Instead, I ended up watching cartoons, playing some video games, and being the victim of Tommy's wrestling attempts. It wasn't my ideal way to spend the day, but since Dad had let me off the hook for being late with only a lecture, I couldn't really complain. I had barely been able to explain away my injuries by claiming a freak work injury, but fortunately Dad had been distracted and hadn't asked any follow up questions.

After lunch, Tommy disappeared into his room to play with his toys which gave me some private time to think. I hadn't been able to sleep because of all the questions running through my head and I needed to get answers. Just when I picked up my phone to call Daniel, the doorbell rang.

"You look dashing today," Daniel said when I opened the door. I hadn't even showered yet and my hair was yanked back in a messy bun. My jeans and t-shirt were wrinkled from wrestling with Tommy and I was pretty sure I had dark circles under my eyes from lack of sleep. All that, plus the bruise and cut on my forehead wasn't going to win me any beauty pageants anytime soon.

"Daniel. Charming as always." I was glad to see Daniel looking and acting more like himself. "Did you have a reason for stopping by or are you just here to comment on my appearance?"

"A little bit of both, actually." Daniel held out the book he was holding. "I came to make sure you hadn't slipped into a coma and to bring you a present."

"Ooh, a present!" I grabbed the book, but frowned when I read the cover. "The Demon Codex? Lamest present ever."

"Well, I'm sorry. It was my understanding that you

like books. I can take it back." Daniel reached out for the book, but I hugged it to my chest.

"No, that's okay. I'm sure it's wonderful." I had been wanting to talk to Daniel all day but now that he was finally standing in front of me, I couldn't think of a single thing to say. "I'd invite you in but we're not supposed to have guests in the house without permission when Dad isn't home."

"Oh, that's okay." Now it was Daniel's turn to look uncomfortable. "I just thought you might want to talk after everything that happened last night."

"Dad doesn't have any rules against guests on the porch," I said, nodding toward the battered porch swing and wondering if it was stable enough to sit on. I settled onto it gingerly and placed the book in my lap, my fingers scanning the embossed lettering.

Daniel gave the swing a skeptical look before perching on the other end. He started talking before I could ask my first question and he didn't stop until two hours later. He told me everything about the Warriors, the Shadows, and the Guardians. He told me more than I could have thought was possible for one person to know. When he was done, I had only one question. "When can I start training?"

"Bennett suggests we start right away," Daniel said.

"Bennett? As in my grumpy boss, Mr. Bennett?" I was dumbfounded.

"Well he *is* the head of the Guardianship." Clearly there were still some things Daniel needed to tell me.

"That's useful information." At least I knew why it had been so easy to get a job. "But if I don't get my powers until I turn 18, what's the point of training now?"

"Your full powers come at 18, but you probably already have some of your powers and you don't even know it."

"Like my visions?" I thought of my blinding headaches that were growing stronger and more purposeful.

Daniel gave me a curious look. "You get visions?"

"That isn't normal for a Warrior?" I couldn't believe that even in my new abnormal world, I was still a freak.

"Warriors have been known to take on unique powers. It's not unusual, but this is the first time I've heard about a Warrior having visions." Daniel frowned slightly.

"So why Provenance?" I couldn't begin to imagine how Daniel and I had been magically drawn to the same town.

"Again, it's a little mysterious. There is a lot of sacred ground in Provenance, which surprisingly makes it an attractive destination for demons." Daniel smiled wryly.

"Opposites attract, I guess. Anyway, it's important to have a Warrior presence in epicenters of demon activity."

"And somehow we both magically ended up here?" I chose to ignore the part about Provenance being a demonic epicenter.

"Not magically. The Guardianship arranged it. They have a lot of connections all over the world and when they want something to happen, it does. Once your move was set in motion, I was notified almost immediately."

"You dropped your life and moved because of me?" That was a lot for me to absorb. "You should hate me."

Daniel shrugged. "I've known the role I would play since I was a child. And I've known about you for almost a year. It was only a matter of time before we would be brought together."

"That doesn't seem very fair. You deserve to have the freedom to choose your own life," I said.

Daniel chuckled. "I could say the same thing to you. Your life has already been planned out too, Alex, and it's likely to be a lot shorter than mine." Daniel stopped talking abruptly as a car pulled into the driveway. I had almost forgotten that Madelyn was due home from cheer camp.

"We should probably wrap this up," I said as my sister walked up the driveway. "I need to go check on

Tommy anyway."

"The Guardianship wants you to attend their meeting tonight. Will you be able to get away?"

Madelyn was on the porch now and she was looking especially spirited. "Company, sis?" she asked with a toss of her hair.

"This is Daniel," I said with zero enthusiasm.

"So it is." Madelyn tilted her head thoughtfully. "I didn't know the rule about no guests when Dad isn't home had been lifted."

"I think it happened at the same time as the rule about minding your own business." Madelyn and I were squared off and ready for battle.

"I should go," Daniel said, making a path between us. "I'll see you tonight?"

"Where should we meet?" I kept a watchful eye on Madelyn, who was clearly eavesdropping while she pretended to search for something in her bag.

"I'll swing by and pick you up. 7:00." Daniel gave Madelyn his most charming smile and she practically swooned. "It was nice to meet you."

Madelyn waited until Daniel's car had pulled away before she started laughing.

"What's so funny?" I said.

"Oh, nothing. I was just picturing Dad's reaction

when you introduce him to Daniel tonight." Madelyn giggled again.

"Don't be so juvenile. I dated Josh for a year and Dad was fine with it." I didn't bother mentioning that it had taken him a few months to warm up to the idea of his daughter dating.

"Yeah, but that was Josh. He was harmless. But Daniel…" Madelyn pursed her lips while she tried to organize her thoughts. "Daniel is the guy you don't take home to meet your dad."

I wondered what Madelyn would say if she ever met Eli. Compared to him, Daniel was downright angelic. "You are being ridiculous. Besides, we aren't even dating. Daniel and I are just friends."

"Sure, you are." Madelyn waggled her eyebrows at me and we both laughed.

"It's your turn to cook dinner tonight," I reminded her as we went inside.

"Fine, but it's your turn to do the dishes."

I spent a good hour or so trying to think of a way to make my escape with Daniel and avoid awkward introductions with Dad. I thought about saying it was Cadence picking me up and then waiting by the curb, but I knew that would only make Dad suspicious. I even thought about calling Daniel and telling him I would meet him elsewhere, but he was in hyper-protective mode after the attack so I was stuck with him as my driver.

"Who is picking you up?" Dad asked as I waited anxiously by the front door.

"A friend from school." I had told him that a group of kids were going to the movies. I didn't like lying to him, but there was no way I could tell him the truth.

"I would hope it's a friend. I would be a little concerned if an enemy was picking you up." Dad was trying to be "cool dad" by making poor attempts at jokes, likely to assuage the guilt he was still feeling over uprooting our lives. "Does your friend have a name?"

I briefly wondered if the name Danny was androgynous enough to eliminate any follow up questions. I took some solace in the fact that worrying so much about my father's reaction to Daniel was lessening the amount of worrying I could do about meeting with the Guardianship.

"His name is Daniel," I said much more confidently than I felt. Daniel's car had pulled into the driveway and I reached out to yank open the door.

"Hold up." Dad had been sitting comfortably on the couch while he watched me squirm, but now he was on his feet. "You will wait for this young man to come to the door for proper introductions."

I groaned but didn't argue. Daniel was already on the

porch anyway, so I waited until he knocked and then opened the door. "My dad wants to meet you," I said with a roll of my eyes.

The introductions were relatively painless. Daniel turned on the charm and Dad refrained from asking too many questions.

"Home by midnight," he reminded me on my way out. I was certainly hoping I wouldn't be interrogated by the Guardianship for longer than five hours.

"The bookstore? Seriously? This is where the Guardianship meets?" I said, staring at the dark spot where the Shadow had disappeared last night.

"What's a secret demon fighting group without a secret meeting room?" Daniel fitted a key into the lock and let us inside.

"Nobody's here," I observed as I looked around the empty store. At least a dozen cars were parked in the lot, but there wasn't a single person in sight.

"Are you sure about that?" Daniel walked over to the wall behind the register and lifted the corner of the painting that hung there. That simple maneuver caused the entire wall to swing open, revealing a hidden room. My mouth dropped open in surprise.

"That's been there this whole time?" I thought about all the times I had stood at the register not knowing the wall behind me was actually a secret door.

"They're waiting for us," Daniel said, urging my forward. The room on the other side of the wall was bigger than I would've thought was possible.

"You're late," Bennett greeted us from the head of the oversized table that spanned the length of the room. He was joined by about two dozen other disgruntled looking men and women. "Please be seated so we can begin."

I could feel eyes watching me as I followed Daniel to the only two open seats. We were barely seated before Bennett started the meeting. Most of what was discussed was beyond my comprehension. I perked up a little when they began to talk about some of the other Warriors, but they didn't go into a lot of detail about them. I kept waiting for Bennett to direct his attention to me, but he seemed perfectly content to focus on anything and everything else.

I didn't realize that I had been tapping my foot until Daniel bumped my knee with his. He gave me a quick wink and I suddenly didn't feel quite so nervous. The distraction prevented me from realizing that the room's attention had turned to me.

"Alexandra Garretty is the newest member of the Warrior coalition. Welcome, Alex." Bennett paused to allow the other Guardians time to murmur their own greetings. He then launched into a speech about the importance of the Guardianship in training the Warriors. He also talked about what an honor it was to be chosen as a Warrior. I wanted to tell him I didn't need the pep talk, that I was already on board. Bennett finished his speech and dismissed the group.

"Alex, one more thing," Bennett said as the Guardians filed from the room. "I know that you have been through a lot lately, and many things are probably still confusing to you."

I suddenly had no idea how to talk to Bennett. He wasn't just my odd boss anymore. "That's true," I said.

"You should know that we are here to help you, Alex. All of us." Bennett peered at me over his glasses. "These next few months are not going to be easy. We will be testing you mentally and physically. You will be asked to do things you can't even imagine. Your life will be put in danger and there is a very good chance you will not live past the age of 20. But you should always remember that none of that will be in vain. This is your destiny."

CHAPTER NINE

"How can you possibly say its lame? You haven't even seen it yet!" Baxter pounded his hand on the table, bouncing my lunch into the air.

"I saw the first two movies, so I think I can pretty safely assume the third one will be equally lame." Cadence calmly took a bite of pasta.

"Alex, back me up on this." Baxter tossed a straw at my head.

"I'm sorry, I stopped listening ten minutes ago." I turned back to my chemistry homework. Between school, work, and my new Warrior training schedule, I had managed to fall behind in nearly all of my classes.

"You might be the worst friend ever," Bax declared, tossing his fork onto his plate.

"Fine. I'm listening." I put down my pen and looked up.

"I was just explaining to Cadence that we need to go see *Possession 3* tonight."

"I've gotta go with Cade on this one. Lame." I shrugged apologetically.

"You hang out in bookstores for fun. Your lameness

radar is clearly out of whack." Baxter swatted Cadence's hand away from his cookie.

"That's probably true. But it's a moot point. I'm busy tonight." I had a training date with Daniel and a history paper to work on. I didn't have the time, nor the desire, to watch a cheesy horror movie.

"Busy with Daniel again?" Cadence said with a knowing smile.

"Fine, choose him over us. We're only your best friends in the whole world. No big deal." Baxter pouted dramatically.

"I would gladly hang out with you if you want to write my history paper for me." I was feeling defensive because I knew Baxter was right– I had been spending almost all my free time with Daniel. I almost wished I could tell them the truth so I wouldn't have to keep lying about how I was spending my time.

"No dice. Work on your paper tonight, but you aren't ditching us tomorrow night, too." Baxter scooped up our trays. "Your homework excuse won't work on a Friday night."

I watched him drop of our trays and asked Cadence, "He's not really mad at me, is he?"

"Bax? Who knows? He's such a girl sometimes." Cadence was busy copying my chemistry homework. "I wouldn't worry about it. He likes you too much to stay mad for long. Bax is terrible at holding a grudge."

I still felt guilty, so I tracked him down on the baseball field in gym class and agreed to see *Possession 3* over the weekend.

"We should definitely go tomorrow night," he said as we waited for our turn to bat.

"What's tomorrow night?" Daniel asked as he joined us in line.

"Movie night, apparently," I told him. I expected him to be annoyed about me making plans when we had a training scheduled, but he surprised me by saying, "What movie are we seeing?"

Baxter moved into the on-deck circle, giving us a chance to talk in private. "People are talking about us," I said.

"About us? What are they saying?"

"They are noticing that we're spending a lot of time together outside of school." I watched as Bax took a practice swing and the bat flew out of his hands.

"By 'they' do you mean Baxter?" Daniel wore an amused expression. "I wasn't aware spending time together is such a big deal."

"You do remember that we're in high school, right? Sharing the same lunch table can be a big deal around here, never mind that I've been at your house every night this week." I didn't really care if people talked about me, but I didn't like lying to my friends.

"We don't really have a choice, do we? You need to train, and I'm the only one that can train you. We'll just have to accept that people might talk."

"Yeah, I know. I just think people would care less if we weren't so secretive. I mean, I know we can't tell people the truth about our relationship, but maybe if we just admitted to a relationship at all that would shut them up."

Daniel stepped back in mock astonishment. "Are you asking me to be your boyfriend?"

"God, no. Not even." My face twisted in disgust. "Forget I even said anything."

I reached for a bat and started to take my place on deck. "Al, wait," Daniel said as he grabbed my arm. He smiled and lowered his eyes, looking shy for the first time ever. "Will you be my fake girlfriend?"

I laughed and walked away. "You are such a dork."

"Is that a yes?" he called after me.

"Fine. Yes. But I'm not going to prom with you."

A few hours later, I got to further prove my point by punching Daniel in the stomach.

"She hits like a girl," Eli said from his watchful

position on the stairs. Daniel and I had been training in his basement every night, but this was the first time Eli had made an appearance.

"In case it slipped your attention, I *am* a girl." I threw another punch, wishing it was Eli that I was hitting instead.

"She's dropping her shoulder," Eli said to Daniel, ignoring me completely.

"Her shoulder is fine," Daniel barked at Eli. He turned back to me and said, "Keep your shoulder up."

Eli was enjoying his role as supervisor. "She's too scrawny. The Shadows will eat her alive."

I gauged the distance between where I stood and where Eli was seated. I had a good chance of getting there and getting in at least two punches before Daniel could stop me. As if Daniel could read my mind, he said, "Eli, you should feel free to leave at any time."

"Why would I leave? I'm obviously so welcome here." Eli settled in more comfortably.

"You do know that I've already killed one Shadow, right? Not too bad for a scrawny girl," I said hotly.

"Beginner's luck. Besides, that was a lesser Shadow demon. You won't stand a chance against one of the big boys." Eli smiled.

"Seriously, Eli. You're not helping." Daniel looked like he was thinking about hitting Eli, too.

"No, Danny boy, you're the one that's not helping. Playing Karate Kid in the basement isn't going to prepare her for what she's going to face out there."

"You think we should just send her out there and what, let her learn through trial and error?" Daniel had raised his voice, something he rarely did.

"It's not the worst idea," Eli said.

"Yes, it is actually. It is the very worst idea. I'm not sending her out there without proper training." If Eli hadn't been blocking the stairs, I doubted either of them would've noticed if I left.

"You two figure this out and let me know. I have other things I can be doing besides watching you fight." I stepped around Eli, moving slowly so that my body wouldn't touch his as I passed.

Daniel's foster mother, Eve, was in the kitchen and I stopped to talk to her. Eve had been at the Guardianship meeting and I had spent some time with her over the last week. I found myself taking frequent water and bathroom breaks just so I could accidentally run into Eve.

"The training with the boys is going well?" Eve asked with a wry smile. The kitchen was at the head of the stairs and she had heard every word Eli and Daniel had said. She poured me a glass of ice water.

"Those two seem to disagree about everything," I

said, taking a grateful sip of water.

Eve smiled a motherly smile. "They argue, yes. But they always agree on the main things."

"Like what?"

"Like keeping you safe, for one," Eve said. "They may not agree on the strategy, but they both would do anything to protect you."

"Daniel, maybe. But Eli? He doesn't strike me as the protective type. The only person Eli seems to care about is himself."

Eve nodded sadly. "Yes, he can come across as cold. But I know for a fact that he is capable of genuine human emotions. He loves Daniel, that much is clear. And I have seen him care for others as well. He's suffered a lot of loss in his life and that is tragic. It keeps people from getting to know the real Elliot."

I didn't like thinking about Eli as a normal person with feelings. He was much easier to picture as a villain. But if what Eve said was true, it could explain how someone like Daniel could be friends with him.

"I should go," I said after I had emptied the water glass. "Thanks, Eve."

"Any time, darling." Eve seemed to understand that I needed these talks with her. She was more than happy to fill the role of mother that had been missing for me for so long.

I called down the stairs, "Good night, Daniel. I'll see you tomorrow." I added as an afterthought, "Good night, Eli."

The next night, Daniel was back to his usual carefree self. He picked me up for the movie and made a big deal about it being our "first date." I would've been annoyed if he wasn't being so darn cute about it.

"You should know, I always kiss on the first date," he joked when we arrived at the theater.

"You should know, I might punch you in the face." I let Daniel open my car door and took his outstretched hand. "If this really is a date, I guess that means you're paying."

"Nonsense. You're a modern woman who believes in gender equality."

"Isn't that convenient for you?" I spotted Cadence and Baxter at the front of the ticket line and waved.

Daniel did end up paying in the end. He claimed it was to keep up the appearance that we were dating, but I suspected he was a gentleman in his core.

"Wouldn't you rather go to a comedy or action movie?" he said as he surveyed the movie poster for *Possession 3*.

"Of course I would, but tonight isn't about what I

want. It's about how I've been a crappy friend lately and I'm trying to make it up to Bax." I wasn't sure how much goodwill I was actually doing by bringing Daniel along.

"I doubt you've been a crappy friend. You've just been busy living your life. Nothing wrong with that." Daniel followed a group of teenagers into theater two.

"How would you know? Isn't Eli your only friend, and he's not exactly a good standard to gauge friendship against." I remembered my talk with Eve and felt a little bad about questioning our friendship.

"And here I thought you were my friend, too." Daniel placed a hand on my back and guided me to the seats that Bax and Cadence were saving. "Eli is a better person than you think. You should give him a chance to prove it to you."

"You almost missed the previews," Bax said as he moved over to give us two seats next to each other.

"It wasn't my fault," I insisted. "Daniel drives like an old lady."

The previews started before Daniel could defend himself. Halfway into the movie, I regretted caving into Baxter. The movie was about a group of teenagers staying in a cabin in the woods that became possessed by a demon they raised during a séance. I could've used a full night of not thinking about demons.

"You should probably be taking notes for our next training session," Daniel whispered in my ear as the actors on screen tried to use holy water to remove the demon from one of their friends.

"If it's as easy as dumping holy water on their heads I don't think I'll need any more training."

We joked about the movie on the ride home. It had been cheesier than I had thought and that had at least lightened my mood.

"Now don't forget, you can just chant a few words in Latin and all the demons will be sent back to hell," Daniel said as he walked me to the door.

"I still don't see why you were making such a big deal about the Shadows when they are clearly so easy to defeat." I stopped in front of the door and turned to say good night, but I froze when I saw Daniel's face. "What's wrong?"

"We're being watched," he said. He moved me closer to the door. "You need to get inside. Now."

"What? Daniel, is it a Shadow? You need to come inside, too." My eyes darted around the yard, but I didn't see anything or anyone lurking in the shadows.

"I don't think it's a Shadow." His face was tense with concentration. "I think it's a human."

My mind raced. Why would any human be watching

us? "Where is it?"

"It was across the street, behind the bushes." Daniel rolled his shoulders to loosen the tense muscles. "It's gone now, whatever it was."

"Are you sure you aren't just being affected by the movie?" I teased.

"The only thing scary about that movie was how bad it was." Daniel attempted a smile. "Now go inside. Good night."

I went inside and locked the door and then crept over to the window. I pulled back the corner of the curtain and watched as Daniel surveyed the yard. He walked slowly back to his car, taking in everything. He sat in his car for fifteen minutes before finally leaving. I should've felt scared knowing that someone was watching me, but instead I felt safe knowing that Daniel was my Guardian.

CHAPTER TEN

"You did problem three wrong," Daniel said with smug satisfaction as he checked his answers against my paper.

"No, I didn't." I didn't even bother to check it. I was good at trigonometry and was confident in my answers.

Daniel and I were sitting at the kitchen table. He was copying my homework answers while I read through a demonology book I had borrowed from the Guardianship. I was learning all about demons that could liquefy your brain, rip out your heart, and break your bones without even touching you. Dad had taken Tommy to his football game and Madelyn was hanging out at a friend's house. It had taken some convincing, but Dad had finally agreed to let Daniel be in the house while he was gone.

"I'm positive you are wrong," Daniel insisted and I continued to ignore him. Daniel was terrible at math and always copied my work.

"Eek." I grimaced at the picture of a demon ripping the head off of a human victim. "Daniel, what do you know about the Seven Princes of Hell."

"What?" Daniel asked without looking up from his

textbook. His eyebrows were joined together in concentration.

"Daniel. Put the trig away and focus." I snapped my fingers in front of his face. He slammed his book shut and then looked at me with mock attention. "This is important. You told me I had to learn this stuff, so help me."

"Right. Okay," Daniel said and took a deep breath. "The Seven Princes of Hell represent the Seven Deadly Sins. You've heard of them?"

"Sure, like lust, greed, gluttony?" I said.

"Right. Each demon is responsible for a different sin. Like Mammaon is greed, Beelzebub is gluttony. Asmodeus is lust. So on and so forth. If you are particularly susceptible to one of those sins, then you are at risk of being possessed by them. Why do you ask?" Daniel leaned over the table to get a better look at the book.

"No particular reason. I'm just trying to make sure I avoid that guy's fate," I said, pointing to the headless man in the picture. "Apparently, he was quite amorous in his prime since he was taken down by Asmodeus."

"Well, if you had to pick a sin, it's not a bad one to go with," Daniel joked.

I ignored him. "If there are hundreds of demons, how do I know which ones to prepare to fight?"

"You'll know. We can see signs of which demons are

exerting their influence on Earth. We just have to pay attention to everything going on in the world." Daniel shrugged as if to say, it's that simple.

"Great. I'll get right on that." I flipped through a few more pages of the book, trying to find a sign as to what might be in store for me.

"Try not to worry too much," Daniel said as he reopened his trig book. "Demons come in all shapes and sizes, but they can all be destroyed the same way."

"Don't you feel like a hypocrite telling me not to worry when you're sitting there freaking out about some stupid math test?" I said.

"No, I don't." Daniel tossed a highlighter at me and I caught it without looking up from my book. "Demon hunting is easy. This math thing is for real."

"It's simple." I put the demon book aside and reached for my homework sheet. "Remember, Sinx/Cosx= Tanx. Then you use these numbers here and this formula and…" I followed along the work I had done and realized that something was wrong.

"Um. I think I added this wrong."

"Thank you!" Daniel threw his pencil in the air in triumph. "I've been trying to tell you that for twenty minutes."

"Yeah, well, everyone makes mistakes." I grabbed

Daniel's pencil and started to erase my work.

"Oh, so you're not perfect?" Daniel was enjoying every minute of this. "You can fight evil but you can't do a simple math problem?"

"Shut up." I started to throw my calculator at him when the doorbell rang. "I'm going to go answer the door. You, hide that book."

Daniel dutifully scooped up the demonology book and shoved it into his book bag as I left the kitchen. I answered the door expecting it to be Cadence who had said she might stop by for the study session. I almost fainted when I saw who it was.

"Surprise," Josh said, holding his arms out wide. I felt my entire body go numb with shock. Once the feeling in my legs began to return, I yelped and threw myself into his arms. He lifted me up in a giant hug and laughed into my neck.

"What are you doing here?" I demanded when he set me on the ground. "You can't be here."

"I just flew halfway across the country to see you and that's how you great me?" Josh flashed one of his toothy smiles that always won me over.

"I'm serious, Josh. You *can't* be here. If my dad sees you…" I didn't even want to finish that thought. If anyone found out that I had contacted Josh, there would be a world of trouble in store for me. "He's going to be home soon. You have to go."

"Fine. Come with me. We can talk and hang out." Josh was as carefree as ever, not comprehending the seriousness of the situation.

"I can't just go with you. I have company." I glanced over my shoulder to make sure Daniel was still out of sight.

"Company?"

"A friend. We're studying trig." I tried to think of a way to get Josh to leave without Daniel seeing him. But I knew that Josh was stubborn and wouldn't leave without a promise that I would meet up with him.

"A friend? I'm shocked!" Josh's smile slowly faded from his face and I knew that Daniel was no longer waiting in the kitchen.

"Who's your guest?" He asked as he walked up behind me. "Aren't you going to invite him inside?"

"You didn't tell me your new friend was Hagrid the giant." Josh joked as Daniel got closer. He flinched just a little, and plastered on a fake smile. "I can't stay. We can catch up later, okay? I'm staying at the Harrison Motel, room 104."

Daniel was standing right behind me now and I felt him tense as he got a better look at Josh. I saw that Josh was clenching his jaw and his hands were balled into fists.

"Alex," Daniel said firmly, "get behind me."

"What? No, Daniel, this is my friend, Josh." I tried to explain the situation and put a hand on Daniel's chest to calm him.

"He's not your friend, Alex. Get behind me, now."

"Chill out, Hagrid." Josh spat out the words. "I'm not here to hurt her. I'm here to help. She needs to know the truth. And I know I can't depend on you to tell her."

"What does that mean?" I looked at Josh first, but he was staring down Daniel. "Daniel, what's he talking about?"

My hand was still on Daniel's chest and I could feel his heart racing. "I'll tell you once he's gone," Daniel said.

"I'm not leaving you alone with her. You'll twist everything and turn her against me." Josh took a step toward Daniel and Daniel grabbed my arm and tried to pull me back.

"Both of you, stop it!" I wrenched my arm free of Daniel's grip and stepped in between them. "Last time I checked, neither of you is the boss of me. Josh, go back to the motel."

Josh opened his mouth to protest, but one look from me shut him up. "We can't talk here. Daniel and I will be there in a few minutes."

Josh hesitated as he glared at Daniel. I repeated, "Go, Josh. I mean it."

"Okay. I'll see you soon?" Josh finally looked away from Daniel and gave me an earnest look.

"Soon," I promised. I watched as Josh took off in his rental car and then turned to Daniel. "Grab your stuff."

"This isn't a good idea. It could be a trap–" I walked away from Daniel before he could finish. I grabbed the notepad next to the phone and started to scribble a note to Dad.

"Daniel, I'm going to meet Josh. You can shut your mouth and come with me, or you can go home. Those are your only choices."

"You don't want to hear what I have to say?" Daniel was bordering on hostile now.

"Yes, I do. But I also want to hear what Josh has to say. The three of us are going to get together and have a little chat, okay?" I slammed the notepad down on the table and grabbed my bag. "Are you coming?"

Daniel turned without a word and grabbed his bag. He took off down the hall, but stopped at the door. "Fine. But I'm driving."

We drove across town in complete silence. Daniel gripped the steering wheel with both hands until his knuckles were completely white. We took turns glaring at one another, neither of us willing to forgive the other one. Daniel parked the car in front of the motel and shut off the engine. I started to open the car door, but he reached over and grabbed my hand.

"Daniel–"

"Just let me talk for a minute, okay? Just one minute." Daniel waited and I nodded for him to continue. "I know that you think this guy is your friend, or whatever. But he's not who he says he is."

"Daniel, you don't even know him. Are you sure you're not just being, I don't know, jealous? Or something?" I tried to keep my words light to avoid another fight.

"You're right, I don't really know him. I'm just saying, neither do you. He's been lying to you, and there's a good chance we are about to walk into something dangerous. I need you to trust me. I promise to give him a chance to explain himself, but if I tell you we need to leave, I need you to listen to me, okay?" He gave me a pleading look.

I could tell that Daniel was being completely sincere now. "Okay, I'll trust you on this."

"Good." Daniel let go of my hand and opened his car door. "And I'm not jealous."

"Okay. If you say so." I climbed out of the car and

looked around.

"I'm not jealous," Daniel insisted.

"Sure. I believe you." But my tone said otherwise. "I don't see anything amiss. No lurking Shadows."

I started toward the motel, looking for the door marked 104. "This is it," I said.

"Seriously. I'm not jealous." Daniel stepped in front of me and knocked on Josh's door. I bumped him aside as the door opened and gave Josh a dazzling smile. He returned the smile and I heard Daniel mutter, "I'm not."

The seating arrangements took a little work as there was only a bed and one desk chair. In the end, I settled into the chair and Josh sat across from me on the bed. Daniel refrained from sitting and instead leaned against the wall near me.

"I don't know where to start," Josh said.

"Start at the beginning, and tell me everything." I wasn't going to settle for anything but the whole truth.

"The beginning." Josh leaned forward until his elbows rested on his knees. He took a deep breath and let it out slowly before glancing at Daniel. "I take it he told you about the Guardianship? And what you really are?"

"Yes, I know that I'm a Warrior. I know all about the Guardianship and the barrier, and the Shadows. What I don't know, is how you know about all of that."

Josh nodded as he thought to himself. "Okay. This is going to be hard for you to believe, but I'm a Messenger."

"You're a messenger? Like a bike messenger?"

"No, just a Messenger. A Messenger from heaven." Josh waited for my reaction. After a few seconds of me staring at him blankly, he said, "Are you... okay?"

"Yes," I said as I tucked my legs underneath me. I had heard his words, understood them even, but they weren't processing in my brain. I had killed a Shadow demon and read dozens of books on demons and hell, but the thought that Josh was a Messenger from heaven was too ridiculous for words. "Go on."

"Messengers are sent on missions, some large and some small. About a year and half ago, I was sent on what was supposed to be a quick mission. I was just supposed to check in on a girl and make sure she was safe. Then I was supposed to report back to heaven on everything I had seen.

"When I found her, she was safe but she wouldn't be for long. I could sense that the Shadow demons were closing in on her. My mission was over and I was supposed to report back to my superiors. But there was something about this girl that told me I couldn't just leave her." Josh reached out like he was going to grab my hand, but Daniel cleared his throat threateningly and Josh pulled his hand back. "That girl was you, Alex."

Whatever I had been expecting, it wasn't that. My head snapped back and my feet crashed to the floor with a thud. "Me?"

"Yes. When we first met, I was acting as a Messenger. When I refused to report back, I lost my Messenger status and joined up with some other rogue Messengers knows as Rebels."

"What does that mean, Rebel? What are you? Are you human?"

"No, not completely. I am mortal now, but I'm not a real human. I guess I'd say I'm mostly human." Josh sat up straight and stretched his back. "My muscles get sore now, but I'm still stronger than most humans. And I still have some other supernatural powers that aren't as easy to explain."

"Let me get this straight," I said with a frown. "You gave up your heavenness or whatever, because of me? That's ridiculous."

Josh laughed. "I know. But it wasn't just because of you. I saw that the demonic influence on Earth was getting stronger and even the Guardianship wasn't prepared. So, I decided to stay down here and help the Rebels fight off the demons. One way I could do that was by keeping you safe."

"The whole time we were together, it was because of what I am? And you didn't think to tell me?" Normally, I tried not to raise my voice during arguments, but this time I felt justified.

"I couldn't tell you. Your power hadn't manifested itself yet. Anything I would have told you would have sounded crazy at the time."

"Guess what– it still does. This whole thing is crazy and unbelievable. But I'm not a clueless idiot. I've known for a long time now that I'm not exactly normal." I had been getting the headaches since before Josh had come along. I had thought I was going crazy or possibly even that I had a brain tumor. It would have been comforting to know the truth, even if the truth happened to be completely insane.

"I wanted to tell you. I did." Josh fidgeted on the bed. "I just wasn't sure how you would react. And then when I finally decided to come clean with you, it was too late. You had vanished.

"I was so worried when you disappeared. I didn't know what had happened, whether you were safe or if something terrible had happened... I looked everywhere for you. Contacted everyone that I thought might be able to help me find you. I felt like a part of me had died."

I heard Daniel exhale sharply and I knew that he was

annoyed. "Gee, Josh, I'm sorry that you were so worried about me because for me it was a barrel of laughs being whisked away in the middle of the night and bounced around between safe houses before being relocated to the middle of the country only to find out that I have some supernatural freaky powers that likely mean I will end up getting killed by demons before I'm even old enough to drink. This all must have been so hard on *you*."

Josh couldn't have looked more hurt if I had punched him in the face. "You're right," he said in a small voice.

"I can't help but wonder," Daniel said in a thoughtful voice. "How did you end up here?"

Josh looked at me for some clue as to how he should respond. I knew that he wanted to protect me, but it wasn't right for me to let him.

"It was me. I contacted him." I couldn't look at Daniel because I couldn't stand to see the disappointment on his face.

"Damn it, Alex," he muttered. "That was a huge mistake."

"Look, I know it was a mistake. But it's done. It can't be taken back. You and I had been fighting and I was going through all this weird stuff that I didn't understand and I just needed a friend. I emailed Josh. It was wrong, and I know that. But anyway, Josh isn't going to hurt me.

He's on our side."

"So he says. I'm not convinced," Daniel said.

"Look Hagrid, just back off. I'm not here to hurt your girlfriend." Josh was getting angry now. "She's right, I'm on your side. Well, I'm on her side anyway."

"Why don't you tell her the real mission of the Rebels?" Daniel had abandoned his spot on the wall and was leaning over the back of my chair.

"What's he talking about, Josh? What haven't you told me?" I was beyond sick of people withholding information from me.

"Nothing, I swear." Josh held his hands up in front of him in a defensive posture. "I think what Daniel is referencing is this belief that some Rebels have ulterior motives."

"Such as?" I was beginning to see why Daniel had been hesitant to jump on the Josh-is-good bandwagon.

"The Rebels believe it's possible to not just seal up the barrier to hell completely, but also to prevent heaven from coming to Earth as well. Which would mean bye-bye Messengers."

"And you think that's possible? The barrier can be sealed against both?" If it really was possible, I couldn't understand why Daniel hadn't mentioned it.

"Yes. The thing is, it would require an elaborate ritual

culminating in a sacrifice." Josh grimaced.

"What kind of sacrifice?" I didn't get the feeling he was talking about animals.

"You've heard of the Paladins?"

"I read a little bit about them in the Guardianship journals." I vaguely recalled that Paladins were very rare. They were humans that had been created with angel blood. They were ultimate Warriors, blessed with strength, speed, telepathy, mind control, and a variety of other supernatural powers. Only a few known Paladins had ever existed, but their biggest value was that they alone had the ability to close the barrier permanently.

"You know what they are capable of?" Josh was getting quieter.

"They can keep the demons in hell for good, right?"

"Yes. If they do it right, they can close the barrier for good. Unfortunately, none of them have succeeded."

I was still missing an important piece of the puzzle. "What does the Paladin have to do with the sacrifice?"

"The Paladin *is* the sacrifice. If a Paladin is sacrificed, the portal to Heaven is closed, too." Josh leaned forward.

"Why would the Rebels want that?" I still wasn't getting what he was trying to tell me.

"They wouldn't want that. That's the point. But the demons would love to seal off heaven. With the portal to heaven sealed, the barrier between hell and Earth would weaken. Before long, demons would walk freely among humans. If they could get their hands on a Paladin, life as we know it would be over."

"I'm sorry. I'm still not getting this. What does any of this have to do with the Rebels and their ulterior motives?" I was starting to feel a bit dense.

"Some of the Rebels, just a few, believe that a Paladin exists right now and they are trying to find him or her. The demons are also hunting this Paladin. The Rebels want to find the Paladin first. At which time they would destroy the Paladin, preventing the possibility of a sacrifice." Josh's voice had lowered like he was afraid of being overheard.

"Kill the Paladin to save the world?" I was finally beginning to understand.

"Exactly."

"Well, that's not going to happen if I can help it. We need this Paladin on our side, to help us banish the demons for good." I stood up and paced across the room. This talk about sacrificing one of my fellow Warriors was not sitting well.

"I agree completely. I'm not on their side, I promise." Josh stood as well.

"Daniel, why didn't you tell me about this?" I said. He had been remarkably quiet throughout our conversation.

"The Guardianship rarely deals with the Rebels. I didn't think this would become an issue. The Paladin will reveal itself to us eventually and we will bring him or her into the Guardianship. Until then, it's a moot point. We can't find the Paladin until the Paladin is ready to be found." Daniel shrugged matter-of-factly.

"You annoy me right now," I said and started pacing again. Josh laughed for the first time since our conversation began.

"So… what now?" he asked.

"Now, you go back to New York. The Guardianship has everything under control here." Daniel pushed his shoulders back until he was standing at full height. Josh was no shrimp at 6'0", but he looked diminished next to Daniel.

"Hagrid, you really need to chill. I'm not going anywhere anytime soon. My spider-sense is telling me that something is about to go down here and I intend to be here when it does." Josh didn't back down from Daniel's hulking frame.

"Do you know any specifics?" I said.

"Not really. But since I've arrived I've been sensing things stronger. In a couple of days, I should have a pretty good idea of what we can expect." Josh started to say something else, but we were interrupted by the ringing of my cell phone.

"It's Dad. Probably wants me home for dinner." I hit the ignore button. "Here's what is going to happen. Josh, stick around but don't go wandering around town. My dad can't know that you're here. Daniel, we need to meet with the Guardianship about finding this Paladin. He could be the key to this whole thing. And if the Rebels really are looking to kill him, we need to get there first."

"Alex, it's not that easy-" Daniel was giving me a look that said he thought I had no idea what I was doing.

"I didn't say it would be easy. I said it's what we're going to do. And if you don't like my plan, you don't have to be a part of it. Josh and I can work alone." I knew that this last part would get him on board.

"Fine." He shook his head at me, signaling that he wasn't a willing participant. "We'll do it your way, but I'm telling you it's not going to work."

"Well then, I guess you'll have fun saying I told you so." I turned and opened the door. "Let's go. Josh, we'll be back tomorrow after school. Promise me you'll stay put until then?"

"Scout's honor." Josh smiled adorably. "You can trust me."

"I sure hope so," I said as I shut the door.

CHAPTER ELEVEN

"Why are you acting weird?" I asked Daniel the next day in gym class. We were supposed to be playing soccer, but we had opted to watch from the bleachers instead.

"What? Weird? Not me." Daniel stretched his legs out in front of him and avoided my gaze.

"You really don't trust Josh, do you?" I looked around to make sure no one was close enough to overhear us.

Daniel cast a sidelong glance in my direction. "No, I don't."

"Daniel-" I tried to protest, but he cut me off.

"You trust him. I get it. You think he's your friend and maybe he is. But in my experience, his kind isn't to be trusted. So, yeah, I don't trust him. Trust has to be earned, and he hasn't done that... yet." Daniel gave me a small smile that I chose to take as encouragement.

"He will. You might not trust him, but you can trust me. I know that I'm right about him." I decided to take a risk and grabbed his hand. It wasn't entirely unusual since we had decided to convince others that we were a couple, but this time the gesture was a purely spontaneous act of affection.

Daniel sighed a defeated sigh and threaded his fingers loosely through mine. "Alright. This is your call, so what do you want to do about him?"

"I think we should use him. He claims that this Paladin exists and that he can help us find him. We need to find out everything Josh knows, and not just about the Paladin. He knows what the Rebels are planning, and about the portal. And he knows about the Shadow demons and he can help us fight them." I tried to focus on Josh and how useful he would be, but my mind kept wandering back to how nice my hand felt in Daniel's.

"So, we will be spending a lot of time with Josh. Excellent," Daniel said with complete sarcasm. "I need to report to the Guardianship and tell them that he's here. They need to know that he's claiming to be on our side."

"You should do that right away. After school, go see Bennett. I'm going to go back to the motel and see what I can learn from Josh."

"Alone? In a motel? I don't think that's a good-" Daniel's voice was growing loud.

"Stop. You said this was my call, and this is what's going to happen. You might be my Guardian, but we both know that I can take care of myself." I fixed Daniel with my toughest game face and he reluctantly nodded his agreement.

"Geez, you two. Knock of the excessive PDA." Baxter interrupted us as he clambered loudly up the metal bleachers. I couldn't help but laugh at him. He was wearing the standard gym shorts, but his gym socks were pulled up to his knees and a sweatband pushed his hair straight up. The effect was somewhat adorable in a nerdy, juvenile way.

"Is it possible for you to look any more ridiculous?" I asked as he took a seat in front of me.

"I think we both know the answer to that." Baxter grinned his big, goofy grin and I laughed again. "What are we talking about, hmmm?"

"Daniel and I were just discussing your oddly shaped knees." I lowered my voice and said, "Maybe you should consider wearing pants. Or higher socks."

"Hardy-har-har." Baxter groaned loudly. "I'm seriously considering finding new friends."

"Let me know how that works out for you," I teased. Daniel was being more quiet than usual and when I looked at him, he was staring off into the distance with a pained expression.

"Bax, I think your team is falling apart without you," I said to distract him from Daniel's bad mood. Baxter already didn't like Daniel very much, so there was no need to add fuel to the fire.

"Eh. They'll survive. Let's talk plans. What should we do this weekend?"

"Um. Nothing, probably. My dad has to go to some conference for work, so I have to watch my brother and sister." I frowned as I realized that I wouldn't be able to see Josh at all over the weekend. I couldn't risk him being seen by Madelyn or Tommy.

"Don't forget, you are tutoring me in trig on Saturday," Daniel said with a big smile, his mood having brightened considerably. No doubt because he had also realized it would be impossible for me to see Josh.

"Lame. Study plans? Why can't I ever be friends with girls who like to have naked pillow fights on the weekends?" Baxter shook his head sadly.

"What about Cadence? Maybe she has a pillow fight lined up." I tried to lift Baxter's mood.

"Negatory. She has some swim meet out of town." Baxter stood up quickly, sending his hair flying madly about his head. "I'm so over you."

I watched him bound away and wondered what he would say if he knew the truth about me. I may not be the coolest person in school, but my life was anything but lame. Being a Warrior against demons from hell should seriously raise my coolness factor.

Josh's motel room was dark when I arrived, so I

opened the curtains to let in some light. A rerun of *Law and Order* played softly in the background.

"So, dear, how was your day?" Josh asked as he spread out lazily on his bed. I looked at him, taking in his lean, strong body and perfect smile. His light brown hair was cropped short and his green eyes sparkled brightly. He was exactly as I remembered him, and yet somehow, he seemed completely foreign to me.

"Cut the crap, Josh. We have a lot of important things to discuss." I moved an empty pizza box and took a seat on the lone chair.

"You're right." Josh propped himself up on his elbows and his smile turned to a grimace. "Where's your boyfriend? I find it hard to believe he let you come here alone."

"Daniel isn't my boss. I go where I want." I stuck out my chin defiantly and tried not to think about why I didn't correct his boyfriend comment.

"I remember," Josh said with a smirk.

"Stop it," I said with an exasperated sigh. I wasn't in the mood for a trip down memory lane.

"Sorry," Josh said, growing serious. "I've just really missed you these past few months."

I ignored his confession. "What can you tell me about this Paladin?"

"The Paladin we're looking for? Not much. Paladins have to reveal themselves to be found and so far, this one is pretty shy." Josh sat up straight now. "There's a lot of mythology on Paladins in general. They are akin to the holy grail."

"How so?" I leaned forward in my seat, completely focused.

"Well, their powers are supposedly off the charts. Messengers, demons, Guardians, Warriors, Shadows- all these beings have supernatural powers. But Paladins make them look like weaklings," Josh said, sounding a bit awed.

"What kind of powers are we talking about here? Super-strength? Magical powers?"

"Yes and yes. Strength, speed, telepathy, mind control, telekinesis, clairvoyance, plus many other things we don't even know about." Josh was talking fast and his face was flushed.

"How many Paladins have there been? The research I've done says that not many have existed." I had scanned a dozen Guardianship books for more information, but not a lot of Paladin literature existed.

"Written records of at least seven Paladins exist. It's likely that a couple others lived unnoticed. The most recent one died in Europe during World War II."

"How did he die?"

"I'm not sure. The Guardianship should have documentation on it." Josh gave me a curious look. "I'm surprised Daniel hasn't given you this information already."

"I'm sure he was planning on it. He's had a lot to teach me in a short amount of time." I wasn't sure why I felt the need to defend Daniel to Josh. "Are you sure you have no idea how to find this Paladin?"

"I'm working on it. I've been consulting some of my sources and we think the Paladin is at least in this area. Somehow, they are usually drawn to the area where they are most needed. Not sure how that works, but it's to our benefit."

"So… what do we do now?" I tried not to sound annoyed, but so far Josh hadn't supplied me with any useful information.

"Well, I thought I could help you train," Josh said hesitantly.

"Thanks, but Daniel and the other Guardians pretty much have that covered." I realized that I was currently running late for a training session with Daniel.

"I doubt that," Josh said. "They might be training your body, but I can help you train your mind."

"What do you mean?"

"You have weird episodes, right? Headaches,

148

dizziness, and visions?" Josh asked, but it was clear that he already knew the answer.

"How did you know?" Even Daniel hadn't known about my visions until I had told him.

"Believe it or not, Alex, I do know some things. And I can help you handle your visions. I can help you interpret them."

"Okay." I badly wanted to be able to control my visions. I stood up abruptly and headed for the door. "But I can't do it today. I have to meet Daniel. Can we start tomorrow?"

"Sure. You know where to find me." Josh looked disappointed that I wasn't staying longer.

"Until tomorrow, then," I said and we exchanged a friendly smile.

Daniel was only a little mad that I was over an hour late to my training session. He had met with the Guardianship and they had insisted on meeting Josh. I knew that Josh wouldn't be thrilled by the news, but they would probably have to meet eventually anyway so we might as well get it over with.

"You're dropping your shoulder again," Daniel said as I threw a punch at his head that he dodged effortlessly. I threw a left jab at him that he deflected easily.

"Your stance is all wrong. Stay on your toes." Daniel

ducked as I threw another punch at his head. "You're telegraphing your punches; I can see them coming a mile away."

"I know! Back off!" I angrily pushed a strand of hair out of my eyes and glared at him.

Daniel didn't back down. "Well if you know, then stop doing it."

I rocked back and forth on my heels a few times and took some deep breaths to calm down. I knew that I wasn't performing well and Daniel's constant criticism wasn't helping. My mind kept wandering back to Josh and the fact that he was suddenly back in my life. Not only that, but everything about our prior relationship had been a lie. I could feel anger rising in my chest and decided to use it as fuel for my training.

For the next ten minutes, I pounded Daniel with punches. He dodged and deflect some, but at least half landed on their target. I didn't let up until I landed a particularly brutal punch under his jaw that sent him flying onto his back. He lay perfectly still and I wondered if I had actually managed to hurt him. Aside from a few bruises and scrapes, Daniel had always left our training sessions relatively unscathed.

"You alright?" I asked, leaning over him. His eyes were closed and it looked like he was unconscious. I reached a hand out to nudge him in the chest, but he grabbed my arm and yanked me down so that I was lying on my back next to him. My collision with the ground knocked the wind out of me and we both lay there taking deep breaths.

"Don't let your guard down," Daniel managed to say between exhales.

"Do you get off on being annoying?" I asked, landing an angry elbow in his ribs. He gave a halting laugh and playfully rubbed his ribs.

"Only when I'm annoying you," he said, propping himself up on an elbow so that he was lying on his side, facing me. "What's with the excessive anger?"

"I don't know what you mean." I folded my hands behind my head and stared at the ceiling.

"Well, you almost took my head off two minutes ago and you've been even more surly and disagreeable than usual. Did something happen with Josh?" Daniel asked with just a hint of terseness in his voice.

"Nope." Except that wasn't really true. In fact, everything had changed between us. There was a long silence as Daniel waited for me to continue. When I couldn't take the silence anymore, I lifted myself up and faced Daniel. "It's just, what is with people pretending to be my friend only to later find out that they only have interest in me because of this whole Warrior thing?"

"I don't think that's the only reason Josh was interested in you," Daniel said and the corners of his mouth turned downward.

"I'm not just talking about Josh," I said. "I'm talking about you, too. And Lily, for that matter. God, even Bennett."

Daniel sat up completely as he realized what I was trying to say. "Alex, yes it's true that I'm your Guardian and that requires us to spend a certain amount of time together. And I did lie to you in the beginning, but that was only to protect you."

"Well, I feel much better now." I slowly bent my body forward, stretching out my leg muscles. I reached until my fingertips touched my toes.

"Here's the thing. I haven't lied to you since that night you were attacked. I've been completely honest with you, even when you haven't been completely honest with me," Daniel said with annoyance around the edges of his words.

I stopped in mid-stretch. "What are you talking about?"

"Well, you never told me you contacted Josh for one thing." Daniel made himself busy arching his back and stretching his neck. I got the feeling he was avoiding eye contact.

"If you'll remember, that all happened while you were still lying to me, so it doesn't count," I said with my own amount of annoyance.

"Whatever." Daniel stood up in one fluid motion.

I stood up quickly and wished that he wasn't so tall so that I could meet him eye-to-eye. "Not whatever. You just accused me of lying to you."

"I wasn't accusing you. I was just stating a fact. Can we move on?" Daniel took a couple steps away from me.

"You're kind of an idiot." I crossed my arms over my chest to keep from striking him with my clenched fists.

"What?" Daniel was getting angry now, too.

"Before I even knew the truth about you, I revealed everything about myself. I told you about who I really was even though I was putting myself and my family in danger. I told you things that even my best friends don't know and you have the audacity to say that I lied to you?" I could feel my face growing hot and my hands were clenched into tight fists.

Daniel's anger melted away in an instant. He stepped toward me and started to reach his hand out to grab mine, but he stopped just before touching me. He let his hand fall uselessly to his side. "Alex, I'm sorry. You're right, I'm a complete idiot."

"Yes." My fists loosened just a bit.

"I'm just weirded out by Josh being in town. I don't like the idea of those Rebel freaks knowing about you. His surprise appearance has me on edge." Daniel gave me a chagrined smile. "And maybe I'm just a little jealous. Or something."

I tried so hard not to smile back, but I couldn't help myself. "Or something," I said.

"So…" Daniel said, "wanna go watch some cheesy reality television with me?"

At this, I grinned spontaneously. Daniel knew that I had a soft spot for bad reality television and he occasionally agreed to watch it with me even though he claimed to hate every minute of it. "You know the way to this girl's heart."

I practically skipped up the stairs.

"You hit like a girl, by the way," Daniel said, still standing at the bottom of the stairs. I turned and gave him a cocky look.

"Yeah, well, this *girl* knocked you on your ass."

Daniel accepted this as a challenge and chased me up the stairs. I didn't run as fast as my new super powers would allow because part of me was kind of hoping he would catch me.

My training with Josh the next day was much less

playful.

"Deep breaths. In and out." Josh spoke softly and even though my eyes were closed I knew that he was pacing slowly behind me. "Focus on emptying your mind of all distractions."

I had been doing okay with the breathing thing, but as soon as he said to get rid of all distractions I was overwhelmed by thoughts. I kept hearing the soft shuffle of Josh's feet on the carpet. I could hear a car alarm blaring out an obnoxious tune outside the window. I even kept thinking about how I couldn't stop thinking.

"It's not working," I announced, shifting in my meditation pose.

"Stop complaining and focus," Josh thumped me lightly on the head. "Deep, even breaths."

"What is this, Lamaze?" I could hear Josh sigh impatiently. "Fine, fine. I'm breathing."

The next couple of minutes were agony for me as I tried to sit quietly and empty my mind. My body was still a little sore from my training session with Daniel the day before and it hurt to sit still on the hard floor. I forced myself to block out the pain and eventually I created a blank canvas. I didn't even realize it had happened until I felt the stabbing pain behind my eyes. I grabbed my head between my hands and tried not to scream.

"Hang on to it, Alex. Don't lose it."

I was aware of Josh kneeling next to me even though my eyes were squeezed tightly shut. "Go with it. Go with the vision."

I didn't know how I was supposed to "go with it," but I was in too much pain to fight it. I saw the usual bright flash before being launched into yet another vision.

This vision started off just like the others with the bright light and buzzing, but then it changed. I could hear voices and make out blurry shapes. "I can't see clearly. There's so much noise."

"Focus, Alex. Pick one thing and focus on it." Josh was whispering urgently in my ear. I tried to focus on the blurry images, but that only seemed to make it worse. Instead, I turned my attention to the voices. Specifically, I tried to hear what the deepest voice was saying. It sounded more urgent than the others, but I could only understand a few words, "must… should… key…," but then I heard an entire sentence.

"We must find the holy dagger and use it to open the barrier."

My eyes flew open and the vision was gone, but that was of little concern to me. Josh stared at me hopefully.

"It worked." I was slightly out of breath. "It really worked."

I laughed and threw my arms around him. It caught him off guard and we both tumbled to the ground. Josh's head made a gently thud as it hit the ground.

"Careful, Alex. I'm just a fragile human." Josh laughed and rubbed the back of his head.

"We both know that's not true," I said, sitting up and pulling him with me.

"So, what did you see?"

"Not much. But I heard something." I paused to make sure I got it right. "I heard a voice say, we must find the holy dagger and use it to open the barrier. Does that mean anything to you?"

"The holy dagger? It rings a bell. But we need more info, like where to find it." Josh scratched his chin thoughtfully. "And it couldn't hurt to find out who else is looking for it."

I nodded in understanding. "Well then, what are we waiting for? Let's go again."

CHAPTER TWELVE

"Maybe we should wait. I mean, what's the hurry? Josh isn't going anywhere," I said to Daniel as I filed away a Leo Tolstoy novel.

"It's going to be fine." Daniel was leaning up against the bookshelves, watching me with amused eyes as I shuffled my armful of books. "Josh is a big boy. I'm sure he can handle whatever the Guardianship throws at him."

I glared at him before moving on to the next book in the stack. "It's not him I'm worried about," I muttered.

"We are officially closed," Lily said with a flourish as she locked the front door. She smiled devilishly. "Now the fun can begin."

"I hate you both." I filed the last book and dusted my hands off on my jeans.

"Stop with the pity party," Lily said, rolling her eyes. "This is not a big deal. They will meet, they will talk, life will go on."

I hoped Lily was right. I hoped that I was just being melodramatic and that this meeting would be harmless. But I had seen Daniel's reaction to Josh's arrival and I knew that he was one of the milder members of the Guardianship. Bennett had almost completely ignored me when I saw him at the beginning of my shift and I took that as a bad sign.

Throughout the evening, various members of the Guardianship had arrived under the pretext of shopping for books. When no one was looking, they had slipped through the hidden door and into the secret room. A couple of them had smiled at me politely, but most had given me a stern look and a frown. Eve had given me a motherly hug, but that had only made me more nervous. Daniel had arrived about an hour ago and followed me nervously around the store.

"You two should go on back," Lily said, checking the time on her phone. "I'll bring Josh back when he gets here."

"But–" My protest was cut short when Daniel grabbed my arm and guided me to the register. He pulled on the hidden lever and the secret door slid open.

The Guardianship members were already seated around the large table. Some of them were talking quietly while others sipped on water or coffee. None of them spoke to me as Daniel circled me around the table. I took a seat in one of the empty chairs and Daniel sat next to me. I tried to make eye contact with some of the members, but they all ignored me, including Bennett.

"Well, this is just delightful," I said, tapping my foot impatiently. Daniel put his hand on my leg, steadying the shaking. I was about to make another snide remark when the door swung open again and Lily led Josh into the room.

Somehow, his presence calmed me. He looked strong and confident as he strode to the seat across from me. "Game on," he said as he slid lazily into the chair and winked at me. I stifled a smile.

I listened quietly as Bennett started the meeting. Introductions were made and Josh briefly explained his history with me and what he was doing in Provenance. Judging from the reactions around the room, Daniel wasn't the only one who didn't trust Josh.

"So, you want us to believe that your loyalty lies with the Guardianship? You'll have to excuse us, Mr. Reid, if we find that hard to believe," Daniel's foster father, Gale, said.

"No, sir. My loyalty does not lie with the Guardianship," Josh said and several members leaned forward in anticipation. "My loyalty lies with Alex. She's the one I swore to protect, and that's what I'm here to do."

"Son," Bennett said with irritation, "Alex is a Warrior.

She doesn't exactly need the protection of someone of your standard."

"Of my standard?" Josh's face grew dark. "I may not have all of my Messenger powers, but I'm not exactly a lowly human. There are things that I can teach her."

"What kind of things?" Daniel said and I felt him tense.

"You guys have the fighting thing down, I'll give you that. And you have all these books filled with fascinating facts and stories. But I can show her how to use her other powers, the ones you don't even know about." Josh leaned back in his chair and crossed his arms over his chest. He looked perfectly relaxed and I almost expected him to kick his feet up on the table.

"What do you mean?" Daniel asked in a low voice. He was glaring across the table with a ferociousness I had never seen.

I put my hand on his arm both to calm him and to have a grip on him should he do something rash. "Josh has been helping me with my visions. Helping me control them and manipulate them."

"How very interesting," Bennett said and he stood up and put his hands on the table, leaning toward Josh. "What do you know about these visions?"

"The visions are just like any of a Warrior's other

powers. Alex needs to train herself on how to control them. I can do that for her." Josh was answering Bennett's question, but he hadn't taken his eyes off Daniel. "We've made good progress."

"What have you seen?" Eve asked, her calm voice breaking some of the tension in the room.

"Not a lot. We've only been working on it the past couple of days and I'm still learning how to focus. But I've heard quite a bit about the demons' plans for the barrier." I tried not to flinch when Daniel's harsh gaze fell on my face.

"Why didn't you tell me?" Daniel slipped his arm away from my hand.

"There really wasn't anything to tell. The first time, I couldn't make much sense of what I was seeing and hearing. I was only able to understand one phrase. But last night I actually came up with some useful information." I gave Daniel an apologetic look. "I would have told you sooner, but I thought it might be better to save it for this meeting so that the others could hear it, too."

I could tell from the way Daniel was clenching his jaw that he didn't believe me. He was right– I was lying. I hadn't said anything because I knew that both Daniel and the Guardianship wouldn't approve of my training with Josh. I had been trying to think of a good way to broach the subject, but I hadn't come up with anything believable. Except for the truth, of course.

"What did you learn?" Daniel asked after a couple of deep breaths.

"A group of demons are hunting for something called the Holy Dagger. They are going to use it to open the barrier. Have you heard of it?" I looked at Bennett.

"Yes, but this would be the first confirmation we have that it's more than just a myth." Bennett seemed enticed by the idea that the holy dagger might truly exist.

"Well these demons sure seem the think it is real. And they think it is right here in Provenance," I said.

Bennett drummed his fingers on the tabletop and his face twisted thoughtfully. "That is intriguing information."

"One thing we didn't learn is why the holy dagger is so important. What is it?" I was glad that the tension of the room had turned away from me, even if only momentarily.

"It's the ultimate weapon. Legend has it that the holy dagger was used by Michael when he cast Lucifer and the other rebelling angels from heaven. It was placed somewhere to be used to fight the demons should they ever make their way onto Earth." Bennett's chair made a loud screech as he pushed back from the table. He walked over to one of the bookcases and retrieved a large, battered book. He ruffled through the pages until he found what he wanted.

"This is the dagger," he said, placing the book in front of Me. "If what you say is true and the dagger is in Provenance, we must find it before they do."

I looked at the picture of the dagger, drawn to a ridiculously sharp point. The word "dagger" didn't seem to do it justice as its size was much larger than a normal dagger. It was about the size of a sword.

"Agreed," I said, tracing the outline of the dagger with my finger.

"Continue your work with Mr. Reid," Bennett said from over my shoulder. "But until we are confident in his true motives, I insist that you have a Guardian present with you during your sessions. Mr. Reid, we will be watching you."

"Goody. I perform better with an audience." Josh quipped, but he didn't look at all pleased about this new directive.

"If the executive members could please stay, we have some matters to discuss. The rest of you are dismissed." Bennett waved one of his hands, further dismissing us. I grabbed the book and practically fled from the room. Josh, Daniel, Eli, and Lily all followed me from the room with varying degrees of speed.

"Your new friends are all so welcoming," Josh said as we marched across the bookstore.

"Don't start. I'm not in the mood." I flipped the deadbolt and yanked open the door. A blast of cool, fresh air slapped my face.

Everyone walked to their respective cars in silence. Daniel was about to get into his car when he stopped suddenly and tossed his keys to Eli. "Take my car," he said. Eli gave him a questioning look, but climbed into driver's seat.

"Alex, drive me home?" Daniel was already opening the passenger's side door of my car.

"What? Oh, fine. Whatever." I wasn't in the mood to fight. I just wanted to go home, crawl into bed and shut out the world.

I revved the engine and blasted the radio, hoping Daniel would take the hint and not try to start a conversation. His silence lasted about two seconds.

"You told him about your visions?" He asked in an accusatory manner after switching off the radio.

"Yes."

"You shouldn't have done that." He said. I could feel his eyes on me. "Have I done something to upset you?"

"No," I said, honestly. "I'm just not in the mood to do this again."

"Do what?"

"Listen to you lecture me about how naïve I am and how wise you are. I get it. You know best. But this is my life we're talking about, and I'm going to live it my way." I stopped the car at a red light and glanced at Daniel expecting him to continue the argument, but instead he just nodded.

"You're right. I have to let you live your life." Daniel cast his eyes away and said, "I just worry about you, that's all."

"You worry about me because you're my Guardian and it's your destiny to protect me. I get it. Just back off a little bit, okay?" I kept my voice light, but Daniel's face remained tight and concerned.

"No, I worry about you because you're my friend and I care about you. But if you don't know that by now then maybe I'm wrong and we aren't friends." Daniel reached over and turned the radio back on. I stared at him, dumbfounded. A blast from a car horn alerted me that the light had changed. I finished driving the last couple blocks to Daniel's house and pulled the car to a stop out front.

"Are we training tomorrow, or are you seeing Josh?" Daniel asked in a neutral voice.

"I'll come over after school. I'd like to work on sword training if that's alright with you." I figured that if a giant dagger was the ultimate weapon that could end all the madness, I had better be skilled at handling it.

"That's fine." Daniel had opened the door and was halfway out when I stopped him.

"Daniel, wait!" The words came out loudly and in a rush. He stopped and turned back to me, waiting expectantly. "Of course we're friends. I didn't mean to imply that I don't think of you as my friend. It's just complicated, that's all. Because we're more than friends, too. We have this other connection and sometimes it's hard to separate our friendship from our destiny."

"Give it time. You'll figure it out." Daniel gave me one of his perfect smiles.

"Does that mean you already have it figured out?"

"Of course. We both know I'm the brains of this operation." Daniel climbed out of the car, but then he leaned back in. "That reminds me, can I copy your trig homework before class tomorrow?"

Dad left for a conference first thing Friday morning, leaving me in charge for the weekend. I dutifully made sure the kids got to school in the morning, made Tommy a snack after school, and set him up in front of the television like a responsible older sister. For dinner, I cooked up some delicious delivery pizza.

When Dad called before bedtime to check on us, it

took repeated assurances that we were all fine before he would hang up. Saturday morning, after setting Tommy up with a big bowl of Crunchy Yums, I hit the books. I spent equal amounts of time working on my English paper and reading up on the holy dagger.

I could hear Madelyn's music blaring upstairs and Tommy was watching cartoons in the living room. I had set up camp in the kitchen with a pile of books and a pot of coffee, facing the door so that I would notice if either Madelyn or Tommy entered the room.

According to the Guardianship's book, the holy dagger could be used to kill any demon. It could also be used by demons to kill anything from humans to Warriors, which explained why the demons were looking for it. It was most likely hidden somewhere that demons wouldn't or couldn't go– sacred ground. Like maybe a church.

I tucked the book away under a pile of homework and went to Dad's office in search of a phonebook. I figured it was as good a place as any to see how many churches were around. When I couldn't find one on the bookshelves, I opened a couple desk drawers. The first two were empty, but the third one was locked. Feeling curious, I retrieved a set of keys from the crooked clay ashtray Madelyn had made him years ago.

The key slid easily into the lock and I felt a little guilty as I slid open the drawer. Obviously, whatever was inside was important enough that Dad had kept it locked up. But then again, how much of a secret could it be when he left the keys sitting out on the desk? It was almost like he wanted me to see what was inside. At least, that's what I told myself as I retrieved the contents of the drawer.

The first item I grabbed was a manila envelope titled "Research" and it was filled with newspaper clippings. The first several were from eight or nine years ago, tracing a series of storms and odd occurrences around the New York area. A tornado in January, snowstorm in June, and a severe drought. A rash of deadly flus and other illnesses. None of it made any sense to me, and it made even less sense to me why it would all be in Dad's drawer.

I tossed the folder onto the desk and pulled out a small box. Inside were various family photos, all taken before Mom died, and a black velvet ring box. Inside the box was a thin silver band– Mom's wedding ring. I placed the ring back in the box and shut it up tight.

The last item in the drawer was another manila folder. This one simply said Mom's name, "Mary," in thick black lettering. I opened it slowly, afraid of what I would find inside. I didn't expect to find more newspaper clippings. They were also from about eight years ago, but this time Dad's interest in the subject matter made sense to me.

Each article was about Mom's death, but not the story I had been told for all these years. Mary hadn't killed herself. Her body had been found in a dirty motel room almost 100 miles from the city. Her throat had been slit, her body drained of blood, and she had been posed in a "ritualistic" manner. I read through each article carefully, trying to make sense of what I was seeing. Dad had been lying to me all these years.

Underneath the articles, I found a copy of the police report that gave graphic crime scene details including photos. I tried to look away as soon as I realized what they showed, but Mom's eyes captivated me. Her beautiful green eyes were open and empty, completely lacking the life that had always sparkled in them, but they were still mesmerizing. I tore my eyes away from them just long enough to take in the vibrant gash across her throat and the lake of blood she seemed to be swimming in.

"Alex! Where are you?" Tommy called from the hallway. I slammed the folder shut and threw everything back in the drawer.

"In here!" I said, my voice shaking. I turned the key in the lock and then tossed it back into the ashtray. Tommy appeared in the doorway, his curls a tangled mess and a red fruit punch mustache staining his upper lip. "What's up, big guy?"

"Can you make me a snack? I'm hungry."

"Sure thing." I tried to act normal and fortunately, Tommy was too distracted by his hunger to notice that my hands were shaking and my eyes were watery.

I dished up a big bowl of chocolate ice cream and tried not to think about the image of my dead mother. I still wasn't sure what had happened to Mom, but now I knew it hadn't been a suicide. Her death had been at the hands of someone, or something, else and Dad had chosen to hide that from me. I had to do whatever I could to found out who had murdered my mother, even if it meant putting myself in danger.

CHAPTER THIRTEEN

"You know we're not supposed to be alone together," Josh reminded me the following Friday when I stopped by the motel to see him after school.

"We're not allowed to train alone. Nothing was said about us hanging out alone." I knew that even if Bennett had forbidden me to see Josh, I wouldn't have listened.

"It's not that I'm not thrilled to see you, because I am." Josh didn't exactly look thrilled though. We had propped the pillows against the headboard and were watching a marathon of my favorite reality show. "I just don't want you to do anything that will upset the Guardianship. I didn't come here to make your life harder, Alex. I came to help you."

"I know that, Josh. Trust me when I say that just being with you helps me." Whatever had happened between us in the past didn't matter anymore. What mattered was that Josh had once been one of the most important people in my life, and I didn't see any reason why that had to change. "I just wish it didn't have to be a big secret."

"I actually don't mind this," Josh said.

"Maybe not yet. But eventually you'll resent me for

this." I felt terrible for making Josh stay locked away in his motel room.

"I could never resent you, Alex." Josh grabbed the remote and turned the channel. "I take that back. If you make me watch any more of that show, I will resent you."

"Well I guess you're in luck then, because I've gotta go." I hadn't realized that I had been with Josh for almost three hours. I had plans to meet Cadence and Baxter.

"Nothing lucky about that," Josh said looking depressed. I hated leaving him in that motel room, but we didn't have a choice.

"I'll come back. We still have a lot of work to do." I had tried to control my visions on my own, but I was having trouble focusing. Josh helped me focus.

Josh walked me to the door. "He'll be with you."

He was talking about Daniel. "Yes, he will. But I'll come by other times, just me, and we can hang out."

"Promise?"

I smiled when I remembered how we used to seal our promises. I gave him a hug instead, relishing in his warmth. "I promise."

An hour later, I found myself wishing for that warmth when I was sitting on the cold metal bleachers watching a football game.

"This was the best you could come up with for a

Friday night?" Cadence said as she shivered next to me.

"Friday night football games are part of teenage Americana, Cade. You shouldn't try to fight it." I wrapped my hands around the cup of hot chocolate I was holding.

Baxter was completely unaffected by the cold. "Yeah, Cade. Embrace it. It's the playoffs!"

"You hate organized sports," Cadence reminded him. "And jocks."

"Hate is a strong word. I prefer loathe." Baxter clapped at something that was happening on the field. He was the only one clapping, so I had to wonder if he even understood the rules of football.

"What's with the good mood then?" I said.

"What, I'm not allowed to be excited about spending a Friday night with my two favorite teenage ladies?" Baxter pretended to be offended.

"Are you sure you're not more excited about who's *not* here?" Cadence said and at the same time, I noticed someone was watching us. I just caught a glimpse of him in the crowd, but I had seen those golden eyes before and I knew what it meant. A Shadow demon had found me.

My instincts told me to stay put. I knew the Shadow demon wouldn't attack me in a crowd. But another part of me was ready to test my training. I couldn't hide from the Shadows forever. Sooner or later, I was going to have to face them. It was a kill or be killed situation.

"I'll be right back," I said before I could second-guess myself. "Bathroom break."

I didn't have to look behind me to know the Shadow demon was following. I moved slowly past the concession stand, on the lookout for a secluded area. On my way past the bathrooms, I found a pile of construction materials that had been carelessly left out in the open.

As subtly as possible, I snaked out a hand and grabbed a screwdriver from the pile. Even a novice demon hunter like myself knew that the only way to kill a Shadow demon was to stab it in the heart with something metal.

I had rounded the bathrooms and was completely alone. Well, almost alone. "I know you're there," I called to the Shadow that was lurking just out of sight.

"And I bet you're glad to see me," he said as he appeared. He was younger than the Shadow I had killed, and after a second I recognized him.

"Billy?" I gasped, as I recognized my lab partner.

The thing inside of Billy's body smiled, exposing its fangs. "Not anymore."

I began to panic. While I was confident in my ability to kill the Shadow, I had serious doubts about being able stab the body of someone I knew. The Shadow sensed my hesitation and lunged, catching me off guard.

I stepped back and tripped, my head smacking the brick wall behind me as I tumbled to the ground. It dazed me, but the training sessions with Daniel had honed my senses and I managed to roll out of the way as the Shadow reached for me. I kicked my legs into the air, arching my back, and swung them back down. The fluid motion put me on my feet again and this time I was ready for a fight.

We faced off like fighters in a ring. I tried not to look at the Shadow's face. When he lunged the second time, I was ready for him. I lowered my shoulder and flipped him over my back. His body made a loud crack when it hit the concrete.

I pounced on him immediately with the screwdriver gripped tightly in my hand. I was ready to drive it into the Shadow's chest when it said, "Alex, wait! Don't. It's me, Billy."

I hesitated, just for an instant. When I looked at his face, the demon was gone– fangs retracted and eyes back to a normal shade of green. It was just a second, but that was all the time it took for the Shadow demon to strike back. It kicked me hard in the stomach and flipped me onto my back. The screwdriver fell from my hand.

When the Shadow jumped on me, it had returned to its demon form with no trace of the real Billy. I hated myself for falling for its mind trick. I could see the screwdriver just a few inches away and I stretched my hand as far as it would go. My fingers closed around the handle, but it was too late. The Shadow had me pinned to the ground with one hand while its other hand closed around my throat.

I gasped for air and my vision started to go black around the edges. In my mind, I screamed Daniel's name, but the only actual sound I made was a choked gurgle.

"You're not much of a Warrior, are you?" the Shadow hissed in my ear. I closed my eyes and waited for its fangs to sink into my neck. Something deep inside me screamed for me to fight. I didn't even feel my arm moving, but I heard the Shadow scream out in pain as the screwdriver plunged into its heart through his back.

I opened my eyes in time to see the gold fade away and the fangs retreat. Black ooze started to trickle from its nose and ears. The hand that had been cutting off my oxygen supply slipped from my throat and I sucked in the air greedily. With a great effort, I tossed the body aside. I couldn't look at it. All I would see now was Billy's dead body taken down by my own hand. It didn't matter that it had been possessed by a demon because before that it had been a sixteen-year-old boy that I used to sit next to in class.

I was still sitting there twenty minutes later when the

body had faded away to nothing but ooze, the black goo having melted away the corpse and clothing. Somehow, I managed to stumble to the front entrance. I wanted to go home, but I had gotten a ride to the game from Cadence and I couldn't face my friends after what I had just done.

I stumbled out into the deserted parking lot, moving as far away as possible from the cheering crowd behind me.

"Alex!" Daniel rushed toward me. He grabbed my shoulders and looked me over carefully. "Are you okay?"

"I'm fine," I said, even though nothing could've been further from the truth. "There was a Shadow demon at the game, watching me. It attacked me and I killed it."

"Thank God you're okay," Daniel said, not realizing that there was more to the story. He did something unexpected then– he hugged me. Under any other circumstance, I would've pushed him away. I would have been angry that he was coddling me. But right then, I needed a hug. I collapsed against him.

"I need to get away from here," I mumbled into his shoulder.

"I'll take you home." He pulled away, but kept one hand on my shoulder.

I shook my head causing pain to shoot down my neck. "Not home." I couldn't face my family in the state I was in. They would know something bad had happened, not to mention that my shirt and hair were caked with black demon goo. "I can't go home like this."

"We'll go to my house. You can clean up there and borrow something of Lily's to wear home." Daniel steered me in the direction of his car.

I remembered that Cadence and Baxter were still waiting for me in the stands, so I sent them a text saying that I wasn't feeling well and had gotten a ride home. When we got to Daniel's house, I immediately took a shower and scrubbed my skin until it was raw. I couldn't wash away the dread that had settled over me.

Daniel had given me one of Lily's shirts– a pink one with a rainbow dancing across it. It looked ridiculous on me, but I couldn't bring myself to care.

"Are you ready to go home now?" Daniel asked once I had finished dressing. Eve had sensed that I wasn't feeling well and had set me up with a giant cup of tea.

"She can't go home with her hair dripping wet. That would be even more suspicious than a few spots of demon gunk." Eli had been watching me carefully since I had come into the kitchen.

"He's right," I agreed. Dad wouldn't miss something that obvious.

"Of course I'm right. Just like I was right that the best

way to hone your skills was to throw you into the thick of it. A little Shadow stabbing is just what you needed to perfect your attack." Eli looked cockier than usual in his leather jacket.

"Aren't you running late for your date?" Daniel said as he refilled my cup.

"She'll wait," Eli said with full confidence. "They always do."

I was so busy sulking that I didn't even react. That was when Daniel seemed to notice something deeper was going on with me. "Alex and I need to talk," he told Eli, interrupting one of his stories about some poor girl that had fallen into his trap.

"Ah, yes. You guys are in need of some Guardian-Warrior bonding time. I won't interfere any longer. Everyone knows I'm not opposed to bondage." Eli grabbed his car keys from the hook by the door. "You crazy kids enjoy your night. I certainly intend to enjoy mine."

"Sorry about Eli," Daniel said when he was gone. "He brags a lot, but he's mostly just talk."

"I don't care about Eli," I said.

"Alex, what really happened tonight? You're keeping something from me." Daniel pulled up a chair next to me at the kitchen table.

"It was Billy. The Shadow, it was in Billy's body." I shuddered just saying his name. "I killed Billy."

"Oh, Alex." Daniel tugged at his hair. "You can't think like that. Once the demon takes over, the human soul is gone. Forever."

"I know, Daniel. But that doesn't make it any easier." I suddenly felt very tired. "His family is never going to know what happened to him. His parents will spend the rest of their lives wondering and they won't even have a body to bury."

"It's terrible," Daniel agreed. "But it only proves that what we do is essential. If we can seal the barrier forever, we can stop this from happening in the future."

"This is going to be a lot harder than I thought," I admitted.

"Did you really think being a Warrior was going to be easy?"

"Not easy, no. But it at least seemed black and white—demons bad, Warriors good. Tonight just proved to me that there are going to be a million shades of gray I never imagined." I looked at Daniel. "How can I prepare for that?"

"I don't think you can. But maybe realizing it is a big step in the right direction."

"My hair is almost dry. I should probably go home

soon." I fingered the ends of my damp hair. "Daniel, how did you know to come find me tonight?"

"You told me you were going to the game."

"No, I didn't ask how you knew *where* to find me. I asked how you knew to come for me? How did you know I needed you?" It was something that had been bothering me all night.

"I'm sure you've sensed that we have this connection. It's important for Guardians to know when the Warriors they are training are in trouble." Daniel squirmed a little. "This time it was different though. I didn't just sense the danger, I actually heard you call my name. It was like you were inside my head."

"You could hear me?" I said.

"I'm sure I was just imagining it. You were in danger, and I could feel it so I probably just imagined I could hear you." Daniel laughed lightly. "If you were really inside my brain, things could get a little awkward."

"Yeah," I said, but inside I knew the truth. I had called to Daniel in my mind, and he had heard me.

CHAPTER FOURTEEN

Immediately after the confrontation with the Billy Shadow, I was barely able to leave my house. Everywhere I turned, I was faced with what I had done. The news replayed endless footage of Billy's parents begging for any information about their son. I found his picture on fliers scattered all over town, including at the bookstore. The police even showed up at school to question his friends about what may have happened to him.

I tried to hide from all of it, locking myself away from the world and everyone in it, including Josh. The problem was, even when it was just me in an empty room, I was still stuck with the memories in my head. Those were never going away. After six weeks of this inner torture, I finally made the decision to forgive myself.

I knew I hadn't done anything wrong, not really. I had killed a demon, not Billy. I was using the Billy thing to escape from my destiny, but eventually I realized that I had to stop making excuses. The Shadows weren't going to stop hunting me just because I didn't want to be a Warrior. I had to start fighting again.

I showed up at Daniel's house after my six week

break and told him I was ready to train. He never said anything, but he watched me all the time, even more than before my breakdown. Josh simply said, "Finally," and immediately launched back into our training.

As winter rolled to an end, I had killed five Shadows and it never got any easier. Sure, I perfected my fighting technique and I rarely got taken by surprise anymore, but actually stabbing them in the chest still tore me apart inside.

"Why didn't we try this place sooner?" Eli said as we stepped over the shattered threshold to an abandoned church. For the last few weeks, when I wasn't battling Shadow demons, I was scoping out every inch of sacred ground in Provenance, hoping to find the holy dagger before the bad guys.

Eli had taken to joining us on our scavenger hunts. I had protested at first, but now I actually kind of liked having him there. At least he kept things from being boring.

"In case you don't remember, I'm not from around here. It took some time to find this place." I hadn't known anything was on the bluffs besides woods. The church was completely hidden from below and it wasn't until we got up close that I saw how big it truly was. It was going to take some time to search the entire place. "And besides, it's been abandoned for so long I'm not sure it even constitutes sacred ground anymore."

"Why are the sacred places you find so boring?" Eli said, picking up a dusty hymnal. "I'd prefer a haunted cemetery, or even a convent."

"A convent? You would prefer a convent?" I had to laugh at that.

Eli tossed the hymnal to the floor with a loud thud and I heard a scurry of little feet scamper for cover. "All those pure, innocent women in one place? I think that would be slightly preferable to this dump."

"In your mind, those innocent women are also young and attractive, aren't they?" Daniel shone his flashlight at Eli's face.

"I'm going to check the altar," I said. Once Eli and Daniel started teasing each other, they almost always lost focus on the matter at hand. I really didn't want to be searching the church all night.

The altar was nothing more than a slab of wood set on a pedestal. I searched it for hidden compartments but came up empty. When I looked to see what the guys were up to, they had both disappeared. I heard a shuffling noise coming from the confessionals and aimed my flashlight in that direction.

Daniel appeared, shirt sleeves rolled up, and dusted

his hands on his jeans. The light caught the flash of his eyes when he looked at me and he smiled his perfect, crooked smile. "No dagger."

For the first time in a long time, I didn't see Daniel as my Guardian. In that instant, he was just another teenager– albeit an alarmingly attractive male teenager. I felt a strange ache in the center of my chest. Not a painful ache, but it was definitely unsettling. I smiled back at Daniel and my cheeks flushed with warmth. *Oh, crap,* I thought to myself. *You have feelings for Daniel.*

"There is some disgusting stuff going on back here," Eli called from the rectory to the left of the altar. I jumped and dropped my flashlight. When I bent over to pick it up, I noticed a strange etching on the floor.

"Hey, guys," I said, tracing the etching with my fingers, "I think I found something."

Eli got there before Daniel and he dropped to his knees next to me. "Latin," he said when he saw the engraved words.

"Can you read it?" My knowledge of Latin was completely encompassed by the phrase Carpe Diem, and I doubted the church had felt the need to scrawl "Seize the Day" on the floor.

"It's a ward against demons," Daniel said. He had walked so quietly I hadn't heard him approach.

"Showoff," Eli muttered, scanning his light at the area around us. "Is it just me, or does this look like a door?"

He was right. A two-foot square section around the etching was slightly raised.

We worked as a team to lift the heavy slab of granite and push it aside. Even before we directed our lights into the hole, I knew we had found the dagger.

"It's bigger than I thought it would be," Eli said later when we were gathered around the table in the secret Guardianship room. I thought it looked sharper, too. "And, yes, in case you were wondering, that is a phrase the ladies often say to me as well."

"You are disgusting," I said, but my heart wasn't in it. Recovering the dagger had been a huge accomplishment and even Eli couldn't ruin the moment.

"And on that note," Eli said, grabbing his jacket, "I have a hot date waiting for me."

"It's almost 11:00 at night," I said.

"Do you have a point?"

Daniel answered for me. "I believe the point is, she can't be that hot if she's desperate enough to sit around waiting for you all night."

"Do you really have that little faith in me?" Eli placed a hand over his heart.

"Just go, Eli. We can take it from here." Daniel was under the same rush as me.

"I can take a hint. I'll leave you lovebirds alone." Eli made a big deal about winking at Daniel on his way out the door and I thought I saw Daniel flinch.

"Was Bennett thoroughly impressed when you called him?" I asked after Eli had gone.

"As impressed as Bennett ever gets." Daniel wrapped the dagger in a wool blanket and placed it in the locked cabinet at the back of the room. "You did well today, Alex. It turns out you're pretty good this Warrior business."

Daniel's long legs crossed the room in just a few strides until he was standing in front of me. I said, "Well, that's only because I have a pretty good Guardian."

"We haven't been alone in a while, you and me. It seems like lately there's always someone else around." Daniel picked up the book about the holy dagger and started paging through it.

"I kind of figured you were doing that on purpose. Because you're scared of me now that I'm this awesome demon hunter." I said it in a joking manner, but I did wonder if Daniel had been avoiding being alone with me. Eli had been at every training session for the past few weeks, something that had almost never happened when we first started training.

"I don't find you *that* annoying," Daniel joked.

"Seriously, Daniel. Have you been avoiding me?" I took the book away from him, forcing Daniel to look at me.

"Maybe a little bit," he admitted.

"Why?"

Daniel knew there was no going back now. "Alex, when I heard you inside my head that night, it freaked me out. That's not normal Warrior-Guardian communication. I thought maybe we were just spending too much time together. It seemed like a good idea to throw more people into the mix to dilute our connection."

I had to agree with him. It had freaked me out, too, even though we hadn't had another moment like that since. That didn't make it any easier to accept, though. "At least I'm not paranoid."

"I'm not saying I enjoyed it, Alex," Daniel said, taking a step closer. We had never been this close before, excluding our training sessions.

I willed myself not to get hypnotized by his eyes. "I didn't enjoy it much either. Especially the part where Eli was always around."

"I've been thinking it over, and I don't think it was the best idea. If you were ever in trouble again, I would want to know. Even if that means having a creepy telepathic connection with you." Daniel touched two fingers to my temple.

Any willpower I might've had disappeared at that touch. I was pulled to him like a magnet, and my hand was behind his neck before I knew what was happening. His lips were warm and soft against mine, just as I knew they would be. Daniel's arm circled my waist and pulled me closer until our bodies touched from head to toe. Our kisses grew more urgent and I lost myself in them.

When Daniel pushed me away, I was breathing heavy and my heart was racing. "We shouldn't have done that," he said, his eyes wide. "That can't happen again."

"No," I agreed, pressing my fingertips to my lips. My brain understood that he was right, but my body didn't want to listen. "I should go home."

Daniel walked me to my car as always, but he left plenty of room between us and we said good night without looking at each other. Nothing in my life was normal anymore, not even a first kiss.

Something happened the next day that blindsided me even more than that kiss. Ever since I had found the file on my mother's murder, I had been trying to find out as much as I could about the real story. I had snuck back into Dad's office and read every article, every detective's note, and even the post-mortem report. When that had turned up a big fat nothing, I had turned to the internet.

After a month of research and no leads, I had finally mentioned it to Daniel. He was as interested in the truth as I was and he promised to look into it. I had always assumed that I would either learn the truth myself, or hear it from Daniel. I did not expect to have all my questions answered by Jim Taylor.

"What's he doing here?" I asked when I found the deputy marshal seated at our kitchen table at breakfast.

"Six-month check-up," Jim said, drinking his coffee.

"Jim needs to speak with each of us to make sure everything is still on track. You *will* answer his questions honestly." Dad fixed me and Madelyn with a meaningful stare. Tommy volunteered to go first, his fascination with Jim preventing him from being nervous.

I, on the other hand, paced the floor in my bedroom as I waited for my turn. I couldn't tell Jim even a fraction of the truth and I had a feeling he was trained to spot a liar.

"So, how's life been treating you, Ally?" he said when it was my turn.

"Just great," I replied, using my finger to trace the condensation ring from my water glass.

"Do you feel like you are starting to fit in here?" Jim had a pretty calming voice.

"Sure. I've made some good friends. I'm getting good grades in school and I have a part-time job at a local bookstore." I smiled what I hoped was an agreeable smile. "Ally Wilson is a Type A teenager."

Jim wrote something in his notebook. "That's great. I'm happy to hear you are meshing well."

"I'm happy to be able to tell you that."

"And what about your boyfriend?" Jim asked, catching me off-guard. I froze, wondering for a second if he was talking about Josh. Did he know I had contacted my former boyfriend? Did he know Josh was in Provenance?

"I'm sorry. What?" I was no longer playing it cool.

"I believe his name is Daniel? Your father mentioned it to me during his interview." Jim glanced back at his notes.

"Yes, his name is Daniel." I was starting to sweat, literally. I'd had no intention of mentioning Daniel during our little talk.

"Feeling shy?" Jim teased. "Alright, I'll just cut to the chase."

I swallowed so hard I was sure he could hear it. My palms were clammy and I tried to wipe them surreptitiously on my jeans.

"I've known about Daniel long before today," Jim

confessed, leaning over the table. "I've actually known about him since before either of you ever moved to town."

"How? Why?"

"What I'm about to tell you, is just between us, okay? Your family can never know this." Jim flipped his notebook shut.

I couldn't form words, so I nodded.

"Your father was told his life was in danger and that's why your family had to leave New York. But that wasn't exactly true." Jim shifted his chair closer to the table and lowered his voice even more. "It was *your* life that was in danger, and still is."

"Because of the Shadow demons," I finished for him.

"Yes. Once they found you, it was important to get you somewhere safe for a while so you could train with your Guardian. Your father's profession allowed us to be creative about the reason for the move, but the Guardianship was always behind it."

"You know about the Guardianship?" I couldn't believe it. Jim looked and acted his part perfectly.

"I work for the Guardianship. I help them keep the Warriors safe."

"Why are you telling me this now? I already know what I am, and it's not like I had any doubts about you being one of the good guys." I would never have thought to be suspicious of the men that had relocated my family.

"I'm telling you about myself because my role in this whole thing runs deeper than you know. I've known you a lot longer than six months, Alex." Jim took a deep breath. "I knew your mother."

"My mom? You knew my mom?" I was desperate to hear what he knew about Mom. "How did you know her?"

Jim's eyes had glossed over and his thoughts were years in the past. "I was her Guardian."

Suddenly everything I had learned about my mom's death made sense. "She was a Warrior."

"She was. Mary gave it up when she met your dad. She wanted to have a family, and she wanted them to be safe. She insisted on moving to New York and taking his last name to get off the Shadow demons' radar. And it worked, for a while."

"But they found her. They murdered her." I could've killed a hundred Shadow demons right then without batting an eye. I wanted them all dead.

"When I learned what had happened to Mary, I was devastated. The Guardianship thought there was a good chance that at least one of her kids would inherit the Warrior gene, and it didn't take long to figure out it would be you." Jim blinked rapidly and I realized he was fighting back emotion. "I promised the Guardianship I would look after you until your powers started to manifest."

"You were watching me all these years? Why would you do that? What about your own life?" I couldn't begin to understand that kind of selflessness.

"My life ended when your mother's did. She was my protectee, and I failed her." Jim reminded me a lot of Daniel in that moment. "I could still honor her by keeping her family safe."

"She was very lucky to have you as her Guardian." I wiped away a tear from my cheek.

"I have no doubt that Daniel would do the same thing for you." Jim pushed back his chair. I knew that he was right- Daniel would do anything for me.

"I just thought you should know the truth about your mother. She deserves to have her memory preserved intact." Jim slid his business card across the table. "If you ever need anything, ever, call me and I'll come running."

I choked down a sob. "How can I ever repay you for what you've done for me and my mom, Deputy Taylor?"

"You can start by calling me Jim." He smiled, but his eyes were still sad. "And you can kill every Shadow demon you face."

"Deal," I said, making the promise to him, myself, and my mom.

CHAPTER FIFTEEN

"There's nothing useful in here!" Josh slammed his book shut and tossed it on the coffee table. We had invited him to Daniel's place to help with research.

I didn't even look up from my own book. This was at least Josh's fifth outburst of the night. Daniel was having a harder time ignoring him.

"If you don't want to help, leave. Nobody is keeping you here." Daniel was seated next to me on the couch and I hardly had to move to punch him in the arm.

"Play nice," I warned him. "Josh, keep reading. We have piles of books to get through and we don't have time for your petulance."

"Petulance? 50-point word score for the brainiac." Josh grabbed another book from the pile on the floor. "I still think this is a useless exercise though. If nobody even knew this thing existed until your vision, I doubt we are going to find a detailed article telling us how to use the Holy Dagger to seal the barrier."

"That may be true," Daniel agreed. "But right now, it's our only shot."

I sat up straight. "Maybe not."

"No?" Josh was eager for an excuse to stop reading.

"Let's think about this. No one in the Guardianship even knew the dagger existed. But the demons knew. Odds are, they also know how it works." I was annoyed I hadn't thought of it sooner.

"That's great, Alex," Josh said, not getting it. "Too bad we don't have any demons on our side that would be willing to tell us."

"You always were a little slow catching on," I said. I was confident in my plan. "We don't need a demon on our side. I can use my powers to tap into their minds. I can use them to figure out how the dagger works."

"Alex, that's not how your visions work. You've never been able to choose your visions, or target them at particular demons." Josh said carefully.

"I've never tried. But I know I can do it." I was ready to plead my case to Daniel, but it was unnecessary.

"If you think it will work, we should try it." Daniel saw my shocked expression. "What? I trust you. It's your call."

"This is a nice change of pace." I slid to the floor and assumed my standard meditation posture while Josh turned off the lights. We had discovered that I found it easier to concentrate in the dark.

Josh walked me through the usual procedure for clearing my mind. It was second nature for me now and took me only a fraction of the time it had taken in the beginning. The pain lasted only seconds and the blinding light was no longer paralyzing. I could keep control enough to guide the vision. I kept my thoughts only on the dagger and skipped through any vision that didn't apply.

The vision I needed came in loud and clear. Never before had a vision felt so real. A group of Shadow demons were gathered around a wooden slab. The female of the group was lighting a row of candles. I could hear every word of their conversation and it gave me all the information I needed. I was about to tune out when I heard something that made me pause.

"How do we get the Warrior here?" the female demon said.

"We could attack her, but if we kill her before we get her on the altar then the ritual will be ruined." This Shadow demon was old, with graying hair.

Another Shadow demon stepped into view and I saw that he wasn't like the others. His features were more demon that human and his eyes burned red rather than gold. "We don't need to take the Warrior. We just need to take someone she loves. She will come to us without a fight."

"Of course, Malthius. We will do as you wish."

I pulled out of the vision so fast it made my head

spin. "No!" The growl came from deep in my lungs.

"Alex." Daniel was on the floor next to me, shaking me by the shoulders. "Alex, what's wrong?"

"They're going to go after my family," I gasped.

It took some time, but I relayed everything I had seen and heard. When I was done, I finished an entire glass of water and collapsed onto the couch.

"We need to inform the Guardianship," Daniel said. He had paced the floor the entire time I was talking and now he leaned against the window frame, staring outside at nothing in particular.

"What we need is a game plan. If they are going after her family, we need to protect them and the best way to do that is to go after the Shadow demons before they can carry out their plan." Josh was on his feet, too.

Daniel turned from the window looking completely calm. "Of course we have to stop them, and the Guardianship will know the best way for us to take on a nest of Shadow demons."

"I've met a lot of Guardians in my time but you might be the first one that was also a coward."

I pushed myself up and nearly collapsed from the exertion. "Josh."

"We don't have time for this." Daniel walked past Josh and offered his hand to me. "I'm taking you upstairs to get some rest while I convene the Guardianship. They will help us figure this out. Josh, you can stay or leave. I don't care either way. Just don't ever call me a coward again."

I let Daniel pull me to my feet and then turned to Josh. I could tell he was conflicted between wanting to protect me and wanting to do things his way. "Alex," his voice broke. "I have to go."

"It's fine." I was too tired to argue with him. "Just don't do anything stupid."

"Who, me?" Josh's smile was empty. "I'll see you soon."

Daniel helped me to the stairs and waited patiently as I climbed them. I had never been upstairs in the Stevens household and it felt like I was violating Daniel's privacy.

His room was at the end of the hall and I almost didn't make it there. I had to lean on Daniel for the last few feet.

"Lay down and rest," he said, pointing to the bed. I wasn't about to protest. The bed was soft and comfortable. I would be asleep in minutes.

"Daniel, what about Josh?" I was worried he might try to take on the Shadow demons on his own.

"Josh will be fine." Daniel perched on the bed next to me. "He's stubborn, but he's not reckless."

"Daniel, if anything happens to my family, I'll never forgive myself." I grabbed his hand and squeezed it tight. "My mother died trying to keep them safe. I can't let anything happen to them."

Daniel didn't say anything right away. When he did reply, the wall he always had up was down. "Alex, I care about you and I would do anything to keep you safe. I will do my best to protect your family, too, but if it comes down to a choice between you or them, I'll choose you every time."

"I know." I didn't expect Daniel to forget his calling. "Your Guardianness only requires you to protect me, not my family. I get it."

Daniel shook his head in frustration. "You really don't get it. The way I feel about you has almost nothing to do with me being your Guardian."

"Daniel, we can't go down that road. You said it yourself, it can't happen." I felt Daniel's hand slip from mine.

"You're right. Forget I said anything." He started to leave, but I sat up and grabbed his arm.

"Don't go." I wasn't tired anymore. Daniel looked at where my fingers were clutched around his arm and his eyes trailed down my arm, up my neck, and landed on my face. This time, we both moved slow and when our lips met it was tender and sweet. We both grew more urgent and I was aware of Daniel's hands on my body. I leaned back on the bed and pulled Daniel with me. When his lips trailed my jaw and kissed my neck I whispered, "Stay."

Daniel did stay, but only for another ten minutes. We still had life and death matters to address and Daniel needed to contact the Guardianship. I managed to fall asleep for about twenty minutes and when I awoke I was fully recovered.

Daniel's room was dark with just a few rays of moonlight streaming through the open windows. At some point someone, probably Daniel, had covered me with a blanket. I noticed that the room was bare, almost as barren as my own. Daniel had three pictures lined up on his dresser and I stepped closer to see them.

One of them was of Daniel and Lily as small children with two adults that could only be their parents. The second was of Daniel and Eli making tough guy faces. It was the third picture that surprised me. A couple of months earlier, Lily had taken a picture of Daniel and I after one of our training sessions. Neither of us had known what she was doing and the picture was a completely candid shot of us looking at one another.

I didn't realize until I saw that photo in his room just how real my connection was with him. We didn't even have to speak– our eyes told an entire conversation. We were both in deep. It was too late to turn back.

My phone vibrated in my back pocket and I let out a relieved sigh when I saw it was Josh calling. I had been worrying about him since he had stormed off.

"Calling to apologize?" I said as I answered the phone. At first, I heard only silence and then a voice I didn't recognize spoke.

"You must be looking for Josh," it said. "I'm sorry, but he's a bit tied up. Can I take a message?"

My vision came roaring back. Malthius had suggested they go after the people I cared about. I had just assumed they meant my family, but of course Josh was an obvious target.

"What do you want?" I asked.

"You." The voice on the other end was practically a growl. "We will let him go if you come to us. Alone. If you bring anyone with you, the boy dies."

"Where?" I felt rage boiling in my veins.

"St. Mark's Church. You know the location? Oh and, Alex, don't forget to bring the dagger."

I stood frozen in the center of the room while a million thoughts swirled through my brain. I had to act fast- the Guardianship was on its way. I had to get out of the house without Daniel seeing me leave. He would never let me go alone and if I didn't go alone, Josh would die.

I only made it into the hall before I was stopped. "You need to be careful," Eli said. He was standing a few feet from the door to Daniel's room and I thought he must have overheard my phone conversation.

"What?"

"You and Daniel. You need to be careful." Eli tucked his hands into his pockets. "It's easy to let emotions take over, but if you aren't careful, emotions will get you killed. Trust me, I would know."

"I'll take that under advisement." I didn't have time to worry about Eli's traumatic past. I made it past him without further interference and when I got downstairs, I could hear Daniel on the phone in the living room. I turned left to exit through the back door in the kitchen.

I stopped at the key hooks and grabbed the set to the bookstore and another set for Daniel's car. Early, I had arrived with Josh, but now I was going to need some solid wheels to carry me up to the church. The backdoor made a loud screech when I opened it, but I couldn't risk waiting to see if anyone had heard. I ran around the house and climbed into Daniel's car. I just made it down the street when I passed Bennett driving in the other direction.

It took twenty long minutes to drive to the bookstore, retrieve the dagger, and drive to the church. Each minute was torture. My phone rang nonstop– alternating calls from Daniel and Lily. Eventually, I turned it off and tossed it into the backseat.

I was aware there was a good chance I was marching to my death, but that didn't stop me from throwing the church doors open with a bang.

The inside of the church was lit by the soft glow of dozens of candles. The effect was a large room covered mostly in shadows. I didn't have time to be afraid because at the head of the room, the Shadow demons were gathered around the altar.

"Did you bring it?" Malthius' voice came out as a growl. I lifted the dagger and waived it in the air.

"Give me Josh and it's all yours." I walked down the center aisle without hesitating, swinging the dagger like a pendulum. "This was a lot of work to go to for some cutlery."

Malthius laughed. "This isn't just about the dagger, love."

"Color me confused, because I'm pretty sure you went to extremes to get me to bring you this thing." I tried to see around the Shadows to find Josh.

"That's right. I needed *you* to bring us the dagger." Malthius stepped away from the altar and I could see the burning flames in his eyes reflecting the flickering candle glow. But Malthius' eyes weren't the most disturbing thing I could see. With Malthius away from the altar, I could see that the altar was no longer bare. A lifeless form lay stretched across the wooden slab, tied down by thick ropes. Josh.

I started to rush toward him, but I stopped when the Shadows moved toward me in unison. I turned my attention back to Malthius. "You need me, huh? I'm part of the ritual, I take it?" I could tell from the flicker of Malthius' eyes that I was right on track. "Fine, you have me and you have the dagger. Let him go."

Malthius flicked a hand and the Shadows behind him spread out. Every fiber in my body was telling me to run, but when my eyes darted past the altar they landed on Josh. There was no way I was leaving without him.

"So what, you're going to kill both of us?" I could see a large gash on Josh's head that was covered in dried blood. His eyes were closed and his breathing was ragged and shallow.

"You need to be bled to death for the ritual to work. That one over there," Malthius pointed to Josh, "is just for fun."

"So that's the big secret? You need Warrior blood for the ritual?" I clutched the dagger tighter. They might have me trapped, but at least I still had a weapon.

Malthius laughed, showing both rows of fangs. "Not Warrior blood. Paladin blood."

"Paladin blood?" I sputtered over the words. For a second I thought Malthius was saying that Josh was a Paladin, but that didn't make any sense.

"You mean they didn't tell you?" This time Malthius' laugh was completely primal. "Oh, that is classic. The disgustingly moral and just Guardianship didn't bother telling you what you really are. Beautiful."

"I'm a Paladin?" I didn't mean to say the words out loud and they echoed around the barren church.

"Yes, love, you are. And your blood is going to bring down the barrier between hell and Earth." Malthius clapped and spread his arms wide. "Isn't that wonderful?"

CHAPTER SIXTEEN

I didn't have time to think about the ramifications of Malthius' revelation. The demons had surrounded me, blocking any potential escape. Josh began to stir, groaning in pain.

"Now, give me the dagger, child." Malthius held his hand out. "I promise to make this as painless as possible."

"Oh, well, if you promise…" I sounded much braver than I felt. I was more or less certain that I was going to die, but I didn't intend to go down without a fight. I leapt forward and swung the dagger, catching Malthius in the shoulder. He snarled and flung me to the ground, the dagger still lodged inside him.

"You will pay for that," he said, yanking the dagger free. Black blood splattered the ground around him.

I jumped to my feet and attacked again, this time pummeling him in the face with my fists. Malthius barely flinched as he caught me by the wrist and sent me flying. This time, my head smacked against the base of the altar and my vision went black.

When I came to, I had taken Josh's place on the altar. My arms were pinned to my sides and my upper body was strapped down by ropes. My feet were also tied together. I couldn't move, couldn't defend myself, but I had one remaining hope.

I closed my eyes and directed my thoughts to Daniel, begging him to hear me as I tried to send him my location. I had no idea how our telepathic communications worked, but I had to try. I worried that even if he somehow heard me, he wouldn't make it in time.

"I know you're awake." Malthius used the dagger to rap on the altar near my head. My eyes flew open. "Now, now. Looks can't kill, so you shouldn't waste your energy. You are certainly going to need it for what I have planned for you."

"And what's that?" I spat out the words, watching as one of the Shadows placed lit candles on the four corners of the altar.

"The Paladin's blood, shed by the tip of the holy dagger, shall open the barrier between the worlds and evil shall inhabit the Earth." Malthius recited the line from memory. "Simply put, I'm going to open your arteries and bleed you dry."

"Has anyone ever told you that you're a bit of a drama queen?" I tested my hands and found that I could move them.

"I must say, I'm glad you aren't a crier." Malthius watched me struggle against the ropes. "Lie still. The ritual only works if you are bleeding over the altar. I have some preparations to make, chanting and summoning and whatnot. Sit tight."

As soon as Malthius was out of my line of site, I returned to struggling with the ropes.

"Alex." Josh's voice came from somewhere underneath me. I craned my neck and caught a glimpse of him tied up on the floor underneath the altar. "You have a plan, right?"

"Sure, Josh. It involves us both being tied up by Shadow demons. How do you think it's going so far?" I knew that snapping at Josh wasn't going to help, but it felt good to vent. I could hear Malthius and the other Shadows chanting from about ten yards to my left.

"You're doing a bang-up job so far, Al." Josh grunted as he fought against his bindings. "Where's the cavalry?"

"That remains to be seen." I had no idea if my mind calling had worked. "Can you get free?"

Josh grunted again. "Nope. I'll say this for them, they know how to tie up their hostages."

"Thank you, boy," Malthius said, coming back into view. I hadn't realized the chanting had stopped. "Now enough compliments; I need to concentrate."

Malthius closed his eyes and raised the dagger over

his head, gripping it with both hands. He resumed chanting and I looked around frantically, hoping a new way out would present itself.

"Chanting, violence, and a sacrificial victim? How was I not invited to this party?" I recognized Eli's voice and turned my head toward it. He stood in the doorway looking strong and focused. "Is it because I'm not dressed right?"

I expected to see Daniel enter the church, but Eli was alone. He clutched a sword in his hand and swung it loosely by his side. Malthius still had the dagger raised, but he was frozen. The other Shadows hesitated before creeping down the aisle toward Eli. They were only a few feet away from him when I heard a muffled sound coming from the other direction.

Malthius heard it, too. As he whirled toward the noise, I squirmed as hard as I could, urging my body to slide upward. The ropes began to edge down lower. If I could just get them around my waist, I would have enough slack to sit up and get myself free. I heard a faint crash and Malthius growled.

"Didn't anyone ever teach you to guard your perimeter?" Daniel's voice was steady and slightly taunting. "You aren't a very good bad guy."

"We'll see if you still feel that way when I'm gutting

you." Malthius had turned his attention away from me completely. I had managed to slide up far enough in the ropes that I could reach them with my hands and I pulled them down further, freeing my arms. When I sat up, I saw that Eli was fighting off three Shadow demons by himself while Daniel was squaring off against Malthius.

I lifted my pants leg and retrieved the dagger I had slid into my boot. It was small but sharp, and I cut through the ropes with minimal effort. Once I had sawed my way through the ones holding me to the altar, I started on the ones binding my feet. I was hurrying and my palms were sweaty. The dagger slipped in my hand and I managed to slice my finger. It was only a small cut, but it was deep and the bleeding started immediately.

I didn't have time to worry about the cut because one of the Shadow demons turned away from Eli and barreled down on me. I cut the last section of rope, freeing myself from the altar. I landed on my feet with the dagger clutched in my uninjured hand. All the training I had been doing was paying off because the proper fighting stance was habit for me.

The Shadow demon was stronger than the ones I had faced in the past, but I was a better fighter now and I managed to land a firm kick in his chest that sent him flying into the wall. One of the sconces that held a lit candle crashed to the floor. The flame landed on a pile of dusty curtains and immediately caught fire. The Shadow demon howled as his arm became engulfed and I drove the dagger into his chest.

"One down," I muttered as I yanked the dagger out and wiped the black ooze on my pants leg. I turned to check on Eli, but he had already taken out one Shadow demon and seemed to have the other one under control. Daniel was having more trouble with Malthius. He was cornered and bloody, but Malthius was also weaponless. I tried to find the holy dagger, but if Daniel had knocked it away it could be anywhere in the rubble of the dilapidated church.

"Malthius," I called. When he turned to me, his face was pure demon. Wild burning eyes, pointy fangs, and even the hint of horns near his temples. I shook away a shudder and said, "You're not looking so pretty. Are you feeling okay?"

"Alex," Daniel cautioned. But it was too late, Malthius had lost interest in Daniel. He came at me in a fury of speed and strength, launching me into a row of broken pews. The blow almost knocked me out, but I fought not to lose consciousness again.

"Leave her alone, Malthius," Daniel warned. My vision was hazy, but I could see Malthius standing near the altar, transfixed by something on it. He grabbed one of the candles and touched it to the altar. The ground began to rumble and dark smoke filled the air. The fire from earlier was still spreading and it was becoming difficult to breathe. I knew we had only minutes to get away or we would all die. I had lost my dagger when I was tossed and I was going to need a new weapon if we were going to get past Malthius.

As I pulled myself to my feet, balancing on the pile of wood, I closed my eyes and pictured the dagger. I saw it in my mind and then willed it to be in my hand. I couldn't explain why I did it, it was just a feeling I had. If Malthius was right and I was a Paladin, maybe I had supernatural powers that could help. It was worth a shot.

Eli shouted from somewhere behind me and when I opened my eyes, the holy dagger flew from underneath a collapsed piano and flew straight at me. I reached out my hand and it sailed right into my open palm. It was warm in my hand, ready to be used. Malthius was surrounded by the swirling black smoke, arms raised triumphantly and laughing wickedly. He didn't even see me coming until it was too late. The dagger sliced into his chest like it was water.

The fire in his eyes burned out and black blood poured from every conceivable hole. I watched as he sank to the floor and his body began liquefying almost immediately. I still had the dagger gripped in my hand, but now it was ice cold.

"Can I get a little help here?" Josh asked from where he was still tied up on the floor. I had forgotten about him completely during all the chaos. Eli appeared and began to hack away at his ropes with a small knife.

"Alex," Daniel's hand was heavy on my shoulder. "We have to go. Now."

I nodded mutely and tried to follow him, but the room began to spin. The air was almost completely black and I couldn't see where I was going. I felt myself falling and Daniel managed to catch me just in time. Eli helped him drag me from the church and then ran to get the car. Josh grabbed my keys and offered to drive it since I clearly wasn't in any state to be operating a motor vehicle. I leaned heavily on Daniel who was equally injured, but he didn't protest.

"What happened in there?" I said, coughing up the smoke and ash that I had inhaled.

Eli pulled the car directly in front of us and Daniel piled me into the backseat and climbed in after me. He hadn't even shut the door before Eli sped away from the engulfed church. The smoke was heavy enough that it would soon be spotted from the city and we needed to be as far away as possible when that happened.

"What was with all that smoke?" Eli said as he steered the car heavily around a sharp curve.

"Alex, did Malthius cut you when you were on the altar?" Daniel groaned as he shifted next to me.

"No. No you stopped him before he could…" My heart sank. "I cut myself. When I was cutting through the ropes I nicked my finger."

Daniel and I both looked to where my hand rested on the seat. The finger was still bleeding. "Alex, did you get blood on the altar?"

"I don't know. I wasn't exactly focusing on that." I knew that it would've been almost impossible for me to not have gotten some blood on the altar. "It shouldn't matter. I wasn't using the Holy Dagger and the ritual requires my blood being shed by the Holy Dagger."

"Maybe not," Daniel said quietly.

"What the heck does that mean?" I pushed lightly on my ribs and winced in pain. My entire body felt broken.

"It means, your blood plus the Holy Dagger destroys the barrier. But maybe your blood alone can still weaken it." Eli glanced in the rearview mirror and my eyes locked on his.

"A weakened barrier means it's going to be much easier for the demons to pay us a visit." Daniel grabbed my hand and wrapped the hem of his shirt around my finger to stop the bleeding. We were all silent as we pondered what a weakened barrier could mean.

We had turned onto the road leading to the hospital and I would only have a few more minutes with Daniel before we were surrounded by doctors and nurses.

"Did you know I am a Paladin?" I wasn't sure I could forgive him if he had been keeping that from me.

"No, I didn't know." Daniel exhaled deeply. "I suspected it when you told me about your visions, but I didn't know for certain."

"Why didn't you tell me?" The edges of my vision were going dark again and I could feel myself getting pulled under.

"Because I was hoping I was wrong."

"Why?" I was whispering now as I fought the darkness. Daniel didn't answer out loud, but just as I was losing consciousness I could hear him in my head. Or at least I thought it was him, but it could just easily have been my mind projecting what I wanted to hear. Either way, I felt myself smile before everything went black.

CHAPTER SEVENTEEN

When I finally opened my eyes, I was staring up at a bright light. I could hear voices and see hazy figures leaning over me. My brain was fuzzy, like it was underwater. I couldn't figure out where I was or how I got there and my eyes were having trouble focusing. Eventually, I gave up trying to understand what was happening and let my eyelids drop.

The next conscious thought I had was that my body hurt. All over. I couldn't lift my arms and turning my head even a little bit sent pain shooting down my neck. I opened my eyes slowly. The room was dark and it took a few minutes for my eyes to adjust. I could hear a beeping noise from somewhere above my head.

Once my eyes focused, I lifted my head a little to get a better look at my surroundings. I was in a hospital room, that much was clear. The beeping noise was coming from a machine that was monitoring my heart rate. I looked down at my body and saw that my right wrist was wrapped in a soft cast. I used my left hand to tenderly prod my aching head. I felt a bandage just above my left temple, probably from when I had been tossed into the pews. I also discovered another larger bandage covering my left torso.

The sound of soft breathing from the corner near my bed startled me. I had thought I was alone. Turning my head slowly, I found Daniel slouched in an uncomfortable looking chair. His long legs were spread out before him and his head hung back awkwardly. The soft light from the machines lit up the angles of his face in such a way that defined his cheekbones and the crook in his nose. It also accentuated the purple bruising and red streaks from the cut on his forehead.

I searched for and found the switch that would raise my bed to a sitting position. As the bed bent my body forward, I felt an intense pain shooting through my ribcage and an involuntary groan escaped my lips. Daniel was at my side instantly.

"I'm okay," I croaked through dry lips. "What happened?"

Daniel grabbed a Styrofoam cup from the bedside table and guided the straw to my lips. I took a couple of long drinks and then he placed it back on the table.

"Well, first off, you killed Malthius. Your floating dagger trick was dramatic but effective." Daniel smiled faintly. "You managed to almost get yourself killed in the process, too."

"What about Josh? Is he okay?" My memory of the

showdown at the church was beginning to slowly come back.

Daniel's smile faded quickly at the mention of Josh. "He's fine. He escaped with barely a scratch thanks to you."

I was relieved to hear Josh was okay, but I tried not to let it show. Daniel would prefer it if Josh wasn't a part of my life at all, but I wasn't about to let that happen. Regardless of why he had come into my life, Josh was my friend.

"What about the barrier? Before I killed Malthius, I thought I saw something." My brow furrowed in concentration as I tried to remember what had happened at the church and in the car before unconsciousness had pulled me under. I remembered dark smoke filling the air, and not just the smoke from the fire.

"The barrier still stands," Daniel said slowly. "But it was weakened by your blood. Even the small amount that you shed was enough to allow passage."

"How many demons got through?" I asked and held my breath while I waited for the answer.

"We're not sure. A few dozen probably. A handful in the area, and other demons likely escaped around the world." Daniel's eyes grew dark. "We've already received some reports of their activities and other Warriors have been called into action."

"Because of me." I felt guilty and vulnerable. One small group of Shadow demons had been able to overpower me and a self-inflicted cut and small amount of my blood had allowed demons to cross over. How would I ever stack up against a stronger demon? I wouldn't. Any other demon would probably have killed me.

"It's not your fault. You did what you had to do." Daniel tried to comfort me, but his words didn't help. I had done what I had to do for myself, not for humanity. I had thought Josh was in danger and selfishly gone off alone to save him. Now dozens or even hundreds of people would die, some of them fellow Warriors. No matter what Daniel said, that was my fault.

I could feel tears pooling in my eyes, so I closed them tight. When I opened them again, Daniel was leaning even closer and he took my uninjured hand in both of his. My hand was cold between his two warm ones.

"What about my dad?" I asked and my voice cracked. "What does he think happened?"

"He's fine. He's worried about you, but we were able to calm him quite a bit. Josh was kind enough to ram your car into a tree so everyone thinks you were in a car accident. You should try to sleep. We can talk more about it when you wake up."

I could feel exhaustion creeping over me like a blanket. I had barely closed my eyes before it took me over completely. The last thing I remembered was Daniel's warm breath on the back of my hand before he pressed his lips against it.

The next time my eyes opened, sunlight was streaming through the hospital room window and Daniel had been replaced by my very worried looking father.

"What's up, Pops?" I coughed deeply and felt my ribs screaming in protest. He handed me some water and this time I drank it all down in one long gulp.

"How you feeling, kiddo?" Dad looked old to me for the first time in my life. I noticed the gray that was speckling his hair now, and the lines that crinkled in the corners of his eyes. The light dusting of a beard was also an unusual sight.

"Eh. I feel like an elephant sat on me. How long have I been in here?" It occurred to me that I had no concept of how much time had passed.

"This is day number three."

Three days. No wonder he looked so frazzled. Knowing him, he hadn't slept at all since I was admitted. I asked him about Madelyn and Tommy and asked about all the school I was missing. I even asked where Daniel had gone because I knew he wouldn't have left me without a good reason.

"I sent him away. He hadn't left that chair since they put you in this room. He looked like he needed a shower and a few good hours of sleep." Dad's eyes were narrowed suspiciously. "He seems to be quite attached to you."

You have no idea, I thought to myself. The whole Warrior-Guardian bond was impossible to understand, but I knew that if the situation had been reversed I would never have left Daniel's side either.

I spent the morning talking to him, skirting over the whole reason I was in the hospital. I had no idea what Dad thought about the car accident story and he didn't seem to be at all anxious to talk about it either. He kept looking at me with an expression that said he knew more than I would have liked. My suspicions were confirmed when he got ready to go pick Tommy up from school.

"Tommy is still shaken up about your accident. I have a hard time getting him in the car." He looked at me meaningfully. Apparently, he wasn't quite buying it. "Just think how scared he would be if he knew the real story."

I almost spit out the mouthful of water I had been about to swallow. "Do *you* know the real story?" I asked him with hesitation.

"Not exactly." He sat next to me on the bed and looked at me with tired, bloodshot eyes. "But I know about you. I know that you're… special."

"What?" I could feel my mouth hanging open. "How do you know?"

"Alex, did you really think I didn't notice all of the things that have been going on with you. Did you really think I was that oblivious?" he said. I thought about denying it, but he didn't seem upset, just resigned. I nodded my head slowly because it still hurt to move it. "I knew the truth about you before we moved. The Guardianship approached me and told me that you were in danger."

"The Guardianship approached you? With the truth about me? And you didn't think they were crazy?" I found this hard to believe. Dad didn't even believe in God, and now I was expected to believe that he had accepted without question my destiny to be a demon hunter. Not likely.

"I definitely thought they were crazy." He laughed, the first laugh I had heard from him in a very long time. "I still do. But part of me also knew that they were right."

"You knew about Mom, didn't you?" It all made sense now. The folder he kept on her death was proof that he knew she wasn't just a random victim. She had told him the truth about herself, and maybe even the truth about me. After she had died, Dad had tried to protect me, and when the time came that he couldn't protect me anymore, he let the Guardianship take over and move us to Provenance.

"I knew from the very beginning. I didn't believe her at first, of course," Dad said with a sad smile. "But your mother could be very persuasive."

"They killed her because they were looking for me." I fought against a wave of guilt and my lower lip quivered slightly.

"Yes." Dad leaned over and spoke urgently. "But it wasn't your fault. She died keeping her family safe, like any mother would do."

I knew that what he said was true, but it didn't stop me from feeling responsible for her death. And now that I had allowed the barrier to be weakened, I was probably going to die anyway and Mom's death would be in vain.

"I have to leave now to pick up your brother. You'll be okay?" Dad was looking at me with concern.

"Yeah, I'll be fine, Dad." I wasn't just trying to convince him, I was trying to convince myself. He planted a kiss on my forehead before he left and I relished the quiet after he was gone.

I had a lot to think about. I had inadvertently allowed demons to cross over to Earth and those demons were likely hunting me. My very existence could endanger everyone I loved and my blood could be used to open the gates of hell. My mother had also been a Warrior and she was killed protecting me. And now on top of all of that, my father had known the truth from the very beginning.

I was still in deep pondering mode when Josh stopped by an hour later. He walked with a discernible limp and he had a black eye and a busted lip, but that didn't stop him from smiling.

"You look like crap, Garretty," he said as he pulled up a chair next to my bed.

"No thanks to you," I snapped. Josh probably had good reasons for not telling me that he knew I was a Paladin, but I was still mad he had kept it from me.

Josh at least had the good sense to look remorseful. "Yeah… sorry about that."

I crossed my arms stubbornly over my chest and pretended to ignore him. I was beginning to realize that no matter how angry Josh made me, I couldn't stop myself from being glad to see him.

"Alex, stop pouting," Josh said with a sigh. "You know you love having me around."

"Get over yourself," I said, annoyed at myself for being so transparent. "But seriously, Josh, if you are going to be a part of my life you've got to stop lying to me. By withholding the truth about me, you almost got me killed."

Josh sat up straight in his chair. "You're right. I should have told you. I thought I was protecting you, but instead I left you vulnerable to attack. It won't happen again."

I surveyed him carefully. His eyes lacked their usual mirth and I could tell that he meant what he said. I said, "Okay. Good."

"Friends?" he asked.

"Friends." We shook on it and Josh seemed relieved that I had let him off the hook so easily.

Daniel arrived a little later, bogged down with schoolbooks and presents. "Oh wonderful. Josh is here," he said as he sat the books next to me on the bed. The look he gave Josh was pure hostility. "Thought you might want these so you don't fall too far behind."

"Wow, homework. Just what I need to feel better." I took the books and tossed them onto the table and out of sight. Daniel took it as an invitation to sit next to me on the bed.

"I also brought you this," he said as he handed me a small gift bag. I eyed him skeptically and peered into the bag.

"Much better," I told him. Inside the bag was a collection of candy that even Willy Wonka would envy. Daniel said nothing and I realized that he was still staring down Josh. On the other side of me, Josh was holding Daniel's gaze and I could feel the tension in the room growing.

"At ease, soldiers," I ordered and Daniel finally turned his gaze to me. "We're all on the same side, remember?"

"What I remember is how he almost got you killed," Daniel said and I saw that his hands were clenched tightly.

"I'd say that's a bit of an exaggeration," Josh said, equally angry. "If you had been doing your job, she never would have made it to that church alone."

"She never would have gone at all if it wasn't for you," Daniel countered. "Her life is in danger now, because of you."

Josh scoffed and he raised his voice, "You blame me for all of this. I didn't make her a Warrior, and I didn't make her a Paladin. But I have helped her and made her stronger. You know that, and it bugs you because you want to be her protector. You think that if you keep her close to you, you can save her."

"You don't know what you're talking about," Daniel said, but his voice waivered.

"Yeah, I do. Because I used to be you." Josh stood up. "I used to think that I could protect her, but I was wrong. She doesn't need to be protected from her destiny, she needs to be prepared for it."

Josh left the room in a hurry. Daniel and I sat in silence for a while, Josh's words still echoing in our heads. I could feel a pounding beginning deep inside my brain and I rubbed my forehead and squeezed my eyes shut.

"You should get some rest," Daniel said quietly. He hadn't looked in my direction since Josh's departure. "I should go."

"No!" Instinctively, I reached out and grabbed Daniel's arm just as he was about to stand up. "Please, stay. Just for a little while."

I scooted over further on the bed, giving him more room. He paused for a second and then settled in more comfortably next to me. "Okay. Just for a while."

"Talk to me," I instructed him. The sound of his voice was soothing.

"About what?"

"Anything." He began talking about his day at school and I closed my eyes and leaned my head on his shoulder. He stopped talking briefly, but then started again. I was still confused about our relationship and I had no idea what Daniel thought about our make-out session in his bedroom, but just being with him was enough for now.

I could feel sleep pulling me down and I gave into it. It wasn't long before the nightmares came. I was being bled over an altar and the demons were marching through the barrier. My family was there and the demons slaughtered them as I looked on helplessly. Josh and Daniel were there, too, fighting the demons but they were losing. Just as one of the demons was turning Daniel's sword against him, I woke up with a scream. My heart was racing and I felt cold sweat on my forehead.

"It's okay, Alex. You're okay. I'm right here." Daniel was still next to me on the bed and he wrapped his arms around me. I breathed deeply to calm my heart and buried my face in Daniel's chest. The dream had felt so real, more like one of my visions than a nightmare. I had been powerless, unable to save the people I loved.

I could hear Daniel's strong heartbeat, and his chest was rising and falling in a steady rhythm. I, on the other hand, was a sweaty, panting mess after a silly nightmare. Some Warrior I had turned out to be. If a demon found me in this state, I would be dead before I could raise a hand to fight it.

Josh might not have been right about Daniel's true intentions, but I realized that I had been depending too much on Daniel to protect me. And Josh was right when he said that I didn't need to be protected, I needed to be prepared. Prepared to fight and prepared to die.

CHAPTER EIGHTEEN

I spent two more days in the hospital recovering from my injuries. I spent another week recovering at home. In all that time, I was hardly ever alone. Dad took a few days off work to stay with me and when he had to go back, Josh volunteered his services. Dad hadn't exactly been thrilled that I had broken the rules and contacted Josh, but he didn't mind having another person looking out for his daughter. He even found a way to explain Josh's presence to Madelyn and Tommy in a way that invited minimal questioning from them.

Daniel came over every day after school and Lily stopped by almost as often. The school was told that I had suffered serious injuries and was at risk for infection, so Cadence and Baxter kept their distance but made daily phone calls to check in. It was all getting to be a little too much for me.

"There's no way. It's just not possible to simultaneously kill six people," Josh said in disbelief while munching on a handful of chips. I was wedged between him and Daniel on the couch watching a poorly made Kung Fu movie. The two of them were currently playing a game where neither of them would leave if the other one stayed. They were on their third movie of the night.

"It's a movie. It's not real." Daniel sighed loudly and I yawned for at least the twentieth time. "And anyway, I have no doubt that move is possible."

"Oh, really? Would you like to prove it?" Josh put down the bag of chips.

"Boys. Really?" I was growing more annoyed with both of them with each passing minute. "First, that was a string of shots put together to make it look like a seamless maneuver. Second, that move can be done, but not by either of you. And third, you guys really need to leave or I'm going to show you just how possible that move is by using it on you."

Josh and Daniel exchanged a look. "Alright. Point taken." Daniel said. He got to his feet and Josh quickly followed. I walked them both to the door and almost slammed it in their faces as they left. I waited until I heard their cars start and the shuffled down the hallway toward the stairs. Just as I had climbed the first step, I heard a soft knock at the door. I opened it wearily and found Josh standing on the porch with a goofy grin on his face.

"What now?" I asked, unable to hide my lack of enthusiasm.

"I need to talk to you about something," Josh said

seriously. He glanced over my shoulder. "Can you come out here?"

"Fine." I stepped outside and pulled the door shut behind me. My family was upstairs in bed, where I wished I was.

I took a seat on the questionable porch swing and pulled my legs up to my chin. "What's up?"

Josh leaned on the railing across from me with his hands in his pockets. "I'm leaving town."

"What? Why?" Even though he had been driving me crazy lately, I didn't relish the thought of him leaving.

"There are some things I need to take care of back in New York. I've been putting it off for too long, and now's a good time for me to go."

"Why now?" I could feel a tightness building in my chest. I hadn't realized how attached I had gotten to him in his short time in Provenance.

"Alex, you've got this whole life here. This life that doesn't include me anymore." He looked at me with sad eyes.

"That's not true."

"Yes, it is." Josh came and sat next to me on the swing. "You have school to finish and you've got your friends. The Guardianship needs you and so does your family. And whether I like it or not, you have Daniel. Your life is full and you don't need me hanging around, taking up space."

"Josh, no. It's not like that at all. I need you here." I grabbed one of his hands and squeezed it tightly in mine.

"No, you don't. You think you do, but you don't." Josh gave me a sad smile. "You were doing just fine without me. I'm not sorry I came. It was so good to see you again and spend time with you. But now it's time for both of us to get back to our lives."

I wanted to protest, but I knew that he was right. On Monday, I would be going back to school and I wouldn't have much time for him. I also knew that he had obligations back in New York and it wasn't right for me to make him stay. "I'm going to miss the crap out of you, you know that right?"

"Ditto." Josh laughed and messed up my hair. "I'll come back and visit. I promise. And you know if you ever need me, for anything, all you have to do is call."

We hugged then, and I gripped him with all my strength. Josh held on gently so as not to hurt my already fragile body.

"Promise me one thing," he whispered in my ear.

"Anything," I said.

"Don't ever forget who you are. You are a strong, smart, capable, loving, and perfect human being. You are

Alex Garretty, and don't ever forget that."

"I won't," I promised him, even though I wasn't quite sure what he meant. When he finally let go, neither of us said goodbye. We looked at one another meaningfully and he tossed me one last toothy smile. I stayed on the swing long after his car had disappeared down the road.

I slept poorly that night and woke up in a bad mood. I missed Josh already and hated the thought of not seeing him for months. I also knew that I had to find a way to keep my promise to him. After heading out to take care of some errands, I spent the rest of the day pouting in my room. Daniel called a few times, but I ignored him. Sometimes misery just isn't in the mood for company.

A knock on my bedroom door pulled me from my depressed stupor. "What are you doing here?" I asked Cadence in surprise. Cadence was weighed down by various bundles and bags. She marched into my room and dumped everything on my bed.

"Your dad let me in," she said, as if that explained everything. She started emptying the bags.

"Is that a dress?" I was suddenly very suspicious.

"Look, Ally. You've been avoiding your life ever since the accident. Daniel called me earlier and he's really worried about you." Cadence dug into one of the smaller bags and brandished a curling iron. "He mentioned that you are healed and will be back in school on Monday, so I don't see any reason why you can't go to the dance tonight."

"Crap. Is tonight prom?" I had completely forgotten that normal teenage life had continued while I was recovering at home.

"It is." Cadence produced a pair of shoes with alarmingly high heels.

"Are you still going with Bax?" I hadn't been surprised a couple of weeks earlier when Cadence had admitted that she and Bax were becoming more than just friends. "I'm not tagging along to prom as a third wheel."

"You won't be a third wheel. I found you a date." Cadence grinned. "One I think you will like."

"You and Bax are my only friends at school so I have no idea-" But suddenly I knew exactly who Cadence meant. "You said you talked to Daniel this morning?"

Cadence's cheeks flushed pink. "Okay, so this was all his idea. Like I said, he's worried about you and he was afraid if he asked you himself you would say no." Cadence glanced at me shyly. "Is everything okay with you two?"

"Sure." I wasn't sure if that was a lie. Daniel and I had spent zero time alone together since I had left the hospital, so we hadn't exactly had a lot of time to discuss our relationship. "I don't think this is a good idea, Cade."

"Well, too bad. I'm not giving you a choice." Cadence held up a dress and waved it in front of me. "Perfect for you, yes?"

I had to agree that Cadence had picked the perfect dress. It was long and sleek, a brilliant sapphire shade of blue that looked great against my skin tone and red hair. Once I saw my reflection in the mirror, I stopped protesting. "Fine, I will go for a little while, but I'm still not fully recovered so I might need to come home early."

"Whatever you say," Cadence said with a knowing smile. She finished perfecting my look with hair and makeup before getting ready herself. I watched Cadence float around the room and wondered what I had done to deserve such a good friend.

When the doorbell rang, I felt a flutter in my stomach. Dad let the guys in while Cadence and I attempted to get down the stairs without tripping. Bax looked like his usual self in a gray suit with a light pink shirt and bright pink tie with his hair sticking out in every direction. On anyone else the look would have been comical, but Bax pulled it off.

"Looking good, Ally," Baxter said after he had provided the requisite compliments to his date. I grinned, but my smile started to falter as I looked around the room.

"Bax, where's Daniel?" Cadence looked worried.

Baxter busied himself with picking imaginary lint off his suit jacket. "He texted me about an hour ago and said something came up so he's going to meet us at the dance."

I tried not to panic. Daniel wouldn't flake on me, I was sure of that. But if something had come up with the Guardianship, he wouldn't be able to flake on them either. When it came to Daniel, I wasn't sure what version of him got priority– Daniel the guy or Daniel the Guardian.

The dance was being held in the ballroom of the nicest hotel in town and when we pulled into the parking lot, it was a sea of sharply dressed teens but Daniel was nowhere to be seen. My inner teenage girl wondered if everyone was staring at me and judging me for getting stood up. My inner Warrior was plotting what Karate move to use on Daniel next time I saw him.

"What's he doing here?" Baxter said as we walked through the main doors to the hotel. Eli was standing just outside the ballroom, wearing a dark suit and looking especially debonair.

"I have no idea." I headed toward him with determined strides. Whenever Eli made an unexpected appearance, trouble wasn't far behind.

"Alley cat, you are looking ravishing," Eli said with a wicked smile. "I couldn't have asked for a lovelier date."

"What are you doing here?" I was aware that people

were watching our exchange.

"Daniel had something come up and he isn't going to make it. He asked me to fill in so you wouldn't be dateless for the prom." Eli tugged at the lapels on his jacket. "I'd have to say you've traded up."

"You'd be the only one to say that." I frowned at the thought of spending the entire evening with Eli. We had only recently started to be able to tolerate one another. "What came up for Daniel? Is everything okay?"

"Everything is fine. Now, shall we?" Eli offered me his arm and I took it reluctantly. The theme for the night was Midnight in Paris and the prom committee had spared no expense converting the ballroom into a pseudo-Paris, complete with a miniature Eifel Tower.

"It's everything I hoped it would be," Eli said as he led me through the center of the room.

"No one is forcing you to be here." I looked around the room hoping to find a distraction. Baxter and Cadence were in line to get their picture taken and I had no intention of capturing my night with Eli for posterity. "If you're going to have an attitude all night, I'd rather you just leave now."

I marched off to the punch table and occupied myself with ladling the red liquid into a plastic cup. The room was filling up and everywhere I looked, teenagers were laughing and posing for pictures. Meanwhile, I was longing to go back to my bedroom.

I had gone to prom with Josh last year and it had been perfect. We had posed for pictures, eaten a fancy dinner, and danced all night. I flushed as I remembered how we had spent our time after prom.

"I'm sorry," Eli said, putting a hand on my shoulder. "This isn't exactly my ideal way to spend an evening."

He sounded serious for once, not sarcastic like usual. I looked at him cautiously.

"The only redeeming part of tonight is that I get to spend it with you." Eli smiled a warm, genuine smile that made me blush and turn away.

"Stop being ridiculous," I said, hoping he hadn't noticed.

"Fine. I promise to be on my best behavior the rest of the night." Eli flashed the trademark Boy Scout signal with his hand. "Can we go eat now?"

Eli kept his word, chatting and charming his way through dinner. Several girls who generally avoided me became my best friends over the course of the night, though they mostly stared at Eli and giggled obnoxiously at his jokes. I was relieved when Eli insisted we take a few spins on the dance floor.

"Are you having fun yet?" he said as he led me

gracefully around the floor.

"I can think of worse ways to spend my time," I said truthfully. I was surprised to find I had been having an okay time. Eli had been an attentive and entertaining date, but I still found myself wishing Daniel hadn't bailed on me.

"I think this is going to be a turning point in our relationship," Eli said, pulling me closer. "We're not secret friends anymore."

"The cat is definitely out of the bag," I agreed as someone from the yearbook staff snapped our picture. At least half of the couples around us were staring dreamily into one another's eyes or were making out. I wondered if I closed my eyes if I could convince myself that I was with Daniel.

"He really wanted to come," Eli said, startling me from my daydream. "Daniel. He really wanted to be here with you."

"I really wanted to be here with him," I admitted. "But you have been a pretty good substitute."

"Maybe, but I'll never be as good as the real thing." Eli smiled sadly. "You deserve a better date than me anyway."

"Eli-" I hated the look of hurt in his eyes and wanted to say something to make him smile, but he pushed me away gently.

"Looks like you are about to get what you deserve." Eli was looking past me and I turned slowly to follow his gaze.

"Daniel." My heart jumped in my chest. He looked wonderful in his perfectly tailored suit. Eli's hands dropped from my waist and he stepped toward Daniel.

"You made it." Eli didn't exactly look thrilled. "She's all yours."

"Thank you, Eli," Daniel said. Eli slapped him on the back and disappeared into the crowd.

"I thought you weren't coming," I said, feeling self-conscious as Daniel absorbed the way I looked in my dress. The front was low cut and I had to force myself not to tug at the fabric.

"You look amazing," Daniel said with an appreciative smile. "Will you dance with me?"

I nodded and took his outstretched hand. He held me more gently than Eli had, one hand pressed on the small of my back and the other trailing slightly lower. I looped my arms around his neck and was glad I had opted to wear Cadence's heels. I was only a few inches shorter than Daniel and our bodies fit together nicely as we swayed to the music.

"Where did you go?" I asked.

"Nowhere special. I just needed to take care of something." Daniel's eyes were glued to my eyes and I couldn't look away. "I hope Eli wasn't too inappropriate. I told him to behave."

"Eli was fine. Better than fine, actually." I frowned as I thought about how abnormal his behavior had been.

"That's good," Daniel said, but he also seemed surprised. "I hated not being here with you tonight."

"You're here now," I reminded him, relaxing in his arms. "I'm really glad you made it."

"Me too." Daniel pulled me closer and I rested my head on his shoulder. Everyone else in the room faded away and it was just the two of us. Daniel pulled me back to reality when he said, "I went to see Josh."

My feet froze and I jerked my head back. "You went to see Josh? Tonight? Why did you do that?"

Daniel's hand pressed more firmly into my back. "The two of you have a history, and for whatever reason you've decided you want him in your life. Josh and I are never going to be friends, but if he's going to be around all the time we should at least get along. So, I went to his motel to tell him that."

"But Josh is leaving town." I was touched that Daniel had been willing to make the effort with Josh even if it was a moot point.

"I know that now." Daniel sighed softly. "I wasn't the biggest fan of him being here, but I know you are going to miss him. I'm sorry, Alex."

I was sorry, too. Josh wouldn't have been happy staying in Provenance, but he would've done it to keep me happy. Daniel wouldn't have wanted him there, but he would have tolerated Josh for me. Sending Josh away was the right thing to do, but that didn't make it any easier.

"Josh is my past. I need to get on with my future, assuming I've even going to have one." I was painfully aware that this might be the last school dance I ever attended.

"We'll worry about the future when it happens," Daniel said, leaning close. "For now, let's just focus on the present."

I was more than happy to do just that.

EPILOGUE

The night of the dance I dreamt of my mother. I saw her being hunted down by demons and tortured into giving up the location of her family. I screamed out for her to just tell them, but she never did. She was so strong and so brave. She had sacrificed herself for love. When I woke up, I knew what she had to do.

I got up early and headed downtown on an important mission. When I got home in the afternoon, I pulled on a pair of shorts and a t-shirt and laced up my yellow sneakers. I stretched out my body and found that some of my muscles were still tight, but none of them protested very painfully.

Dad was pouring over some paperwork in his office. "Hey, Dad. I'm feeling restless so I'm going to run over to Daniel's."

"Are you sure, kiddo? I don't want you to hurt yourself. It's only been ten days since you were discharged from the hospital." He gave me his best worried-father look.

"Ten long, boring, tedious days," I corrected him. "But, yes, I'm sure. I'm pretty much all healed. It pays to be graced with Warrior powers."

"Okay, then," he said reluctantly. "Just be careful. Don't overdo it."

"Yes, sir." I saluted him and hurried from the room. My body was itching to move.

The sun was out, but the air was still cool and it felt great to jog lazily. My muscles responded with pleasure to the exertion and I picked up the pace a bit. By the time I reached Daniel's street, I was running at full speed.

Daniel answered the door and almost fell over in shock. "What did you do?"

I gave him a coy smile. "Whatever do you mean?"

"Well for one thing, you look like you just ran a marathon. But more importantly, you're blond!" Daniel put a hand to his heart and feigned shock.

"No, I'm Alex." I gave him a smile Josh would have envied and pushed my way into the house. "And I'm ready to train."

Daniel followed me down to the basement, but he hesitated as I started taping my wrist.

"Alex, are you sure about this-" I cut him off by throwing a boxing glove at his head.

"I'm sure. Surer than I've ever been of anything." I looked at him determinedly. "This good versus evil thing is happening, whether we like it or not. And if it's okay with you, I'd like to stop it and not die in the process. The only way that's going to happen is if I'm ready for it. I need you to get me ready."

Daniel considered me for a moment, his eyes locked onto mine. A slight nod of his head told me that he was on board. He started swinging lightly at the punching bag.

"Should we have Eli also help you get ready?" he asked in an overly sweet falsetto.

"Yes. Whether I like it or not, Eli is a good fighter." I was bent over, stretching my legs and when I stood up, I saw that my acceptance of Eli had surprised Daniel.

"You guys go to one dance together and now you're friends?" he asked, still frozen mid-swing.

"Friends may be a stretch. But we are on the same team and that's good enough for me." I walked over to where Daniel stood and gave the bag a sharp jab, testing my wrist. "But you're still my Guardian. No matter what."

"So? What does that mean?" Daniel held onto the bag as I hit it harder.

"Well," I said as I pushed my hair out of my face. "I guess it means that when it comes down to it, it's just you and me."

Daniel smiled. "Good to know."

I let off a series of sharp punches and felt relieved that my wrist was holding up with minimal pain. I had only been out of training for a couple of weeks, but I had already lost some strength in that short amount of time.

"Eli won't be much use to you anyway. You're too good of a fighter. Pretty soon he won't be able to handle you." Daniel was still grinning at me.

"I don't know. I think he handles me just fine." I smiled and stepped back from the bag. "And you think you can?"

"I know I can." Daniel let go of the bag and took a step toward me.

"There's only one way to find out." I held up my fists and braced as Daniel lunged. In top condition, I would have beaten him. But my body was still sore and my endurance was subpar. After just a few minutes of sparring and wrestling, I ended up flat on my back with Daniel pinning me to the ground.

"Enjoying yourself?" he asked, towering over me.

"No," I said as I grabbed one of his arms and used my upper body to flip him off me. I shoved him to the ground and pinned his shoulders with my arms. "I like it better on top." I smiled teasingly at him and he laughed.

We sparred for a little while longer until it became clear just how out of shape I had gotten. As we cooled down, Daniel started talking about a workout schedule for me designed to increase my speed and stamina, and to build muscle mass.

"If we get you quick enough and strong enough, I think we stand a chance." Daniel stretched one of his arms in front of him, flexing his bicep.

"Do you really think we can win?" I tried not to let any fear creep into my voice, but Daniel picked up on it anyway.

"Alex, honestly, I don't know." He stepped in front of me and put his hands on my shoulders. Our eye met and I saw that I wasn't the only one that was afraid. "The only thing I know for certain is that I'm going to do everything I can to train you. I'll teach you everything you need to know. And I'll fight alongside you, protecting you when I can. But in the end, it's going to come down to you. And I certainly wouldn't bet against you."

He was right. I had Daniel, Eli, the Guardianship, and Josh all looking out for me, all helping me. But in the end, everything would depend on me. I would have to be strong enough and smart enough. I would have to be brave enough, in the same way that my mother had been brave. I had to fight for my mother, and for my family.

I didn't know if I could win, but I knew that I had to try. I wasn't going to be afraid anymore. I would prepare, I would fight, and with just a bit of luck on my side, I would survive.

Made in the USA
San Bernardino, CA
31 July 2017